ROOM NUMBER SIX

'Man wanted immediately for confidential job, experience unnecessary, honesty essential.'

Simon Smith was down on his luck and accepted the offer of work with alacrity—it certainly sounded intriguing. He was perhaps a little disappointed to discover that the job was quite ordinary—that of a commercial traveller.

Before he made his first sale, however, he discovered that all was not what it seemed when selling Nugum. Aided by the lovely Milly Brown he became involved a deadly turn of events—and his job proved to be not only interesting, but dangerous as well.

ROOM NUMBER SIX

J. Jefferson Farjeon

·BLACK·
DAGGER
·CRIME·

First published in Great Britain 1941
by
William Collins Sons & Co Ltd
This edition 1991 by Chivers Press
published by arrangement with
the author's estate

ISBN 0 86220 803 3

British Library Cataloguing in Publication Data

Farjeon, J. Jefferson (Joseph Jefferson)
    Room number six—(Black dagger crime)
    I. Title
    823.912

ISBN 0–86220–803–3

Printed and bound in Great Britain by
Redwood Press Limited, Melksham, Wiltshire

FOREWORD

IT SEEMED TO be fashionable in the 1970s and 1980s to pontificate about the 'anti-hero', the little man caught up in the shabby raincoat world of espionage, or in the relentless fight against Kafka's 'they'. The 'hero' in Greene's *Our Man in Havana* (1958) might well sell plans of vacuum cleaners to enemy agents in lieu of electronic gadgetry—but we can trace the cult even further back.

Think about the great film comedians: Laurel and Hardy eternally fighting against the foes; Charlie Chaplin, the little tramp; Harry Langdon or Harold Lloyd with his lensless glasses to name but a few. In the 1930s the great *Daily Express* cartoonist Strube invented his 'little man' with an umbrella, courageously fighting the world. Bob Hope completely changed the notion of film horror with his inimitable *The Cat and the Canary* (the third version) and *The Ghost Breakers*, and when the world of 'Silly Assery' had come alive in the 1920s it was again the unlikely hero who won every time.

J. Jefferson Farjeon was a prolific crime writer whose works included *The 5:18 Mystery* (a railway story of 1929); *Dead Man's Heath* and *Fancy Dress Ball*, both of the 1940s; and this present title which, although published in 1941, was obviously based on a pre-war England with no mention of war looming. Farjeon also wrote historical romances and reviews—once upsetting Sidney Horler, the very pro-English writer, by describing his heroines as 'too vapid'.

Farjeon's mother was the daughter of the great American actor Joseph Jefferson (of Rip Van Winkle fame), while his father was B. L. Farjeon, an eccentric and well-known crime writer and journalist. Other members of this colourful family also included Eleanor Farjeon who wrote *Nursery Rhymes of*

London Town and the great Herbert 'Bertie' Farjeon who wrote the *Nine Sharp Revue*. Whilst writing this foreword I met the daughter of our author, Joan Jefferson Farjeon, who explained that there had been four children: Joseph (her own father), Harry, Eleanor and Bertie. Her father achieved his ambition in writing more books than *his* father—ninety-two to the latter's ninety-one!

The hero of *Room Number Six* is Simon Smith and the heroine a much more resourceful Milly Brown—what ordinary names! Such use of simple names may have come about from the influence of Repertory Theatre in which many plays had unnamed characters—just look at the cast of an Elmer Rice play. The same trend can also be seen in modern opera. Simon takes the job of commercial traveller, aided by the much more intelligent and dominating Milly, and finds himself travelling to hotels of the 'commercial' type, selling Nugum glue. He meets a strange collection of nightly visitors including a thug, a vamp, a strange clergyman and a bullying negro and finds himself mixed up in a murder in which the body is found in his hotel room cupboard. The police are all rather easy-going—the Inspector dons disguises, and guns seem easily available.

The story is ingenious and the dialogue light-hearted as Simon and Milly drive through Hertfordshire towns with pseudonymous names, to solve the mystery and live happily ever after. We know they will, of course, with their first kiss, in the best Hollywood and Elstree traditions, on the last page of the book. Indeed this would have made a good pre-war English film comedy-thriller with, say, George Formby as Simon. Of course there is no police computer nor low-flying helicopters to take away the fun—but neither were they around when Richard Hannay fled across the moor in *The Thirty-Nine Steps* or Cary Grant escaped the enemy in Hitchcock's *North by Northwest*—two very different types of hero.

What a pleasure it is to re-introduce such a happy crime story to all readers, like the famous stage show used to advertise—the sort that any child can offer safely to his parents!

JOHN KENNEDY MELLING

John Kennedy Melling, Black Dagger editor, numbers show business amongst his many interests, with three books written on theatre, a large Ephemera Collection often used by other writers and the BBC, and two years' broadcasting on the BBC Radio *Movie-Go-Round* programme.

THE BLACK DAGGER CRIME SERIES

The Black Dagger Crime series is a result of a joint effort between Chivers Press and a sub-committee of the Crime Writers' Association, consisting of Marian Babson, Peter Chambers and chaired by John Kennedy Melling. It is designed to select outstanding examples of every type of detective story, so that enthusiasts will have the opportunity to read once more classics that have been scarce for years, while at the same time introducing them to a new generation who have not previously had the chance to enjoy them.

Contents

CHAPTER ONE

COFFEE FOR TWO

THE FIRST MEETING between Simon Smith and Milly Brown occurred in the unromantic bareness of a public library, and for a while they paid no attention to each other. They were far too busy studying advertisement columns, he of the *Daily Telegraph*, she of *The Times*. But when he suddenly found himself sitting on the floor at the foot of his stand, while the paper on which he had been copying an address floated out of his hand towards her, he became rather painfully conscious of the attractive eyes that stared at him in astonishment—an astonishment he shared, for he did not know why he had suddenly sat down on the floor.

" I say ! Are you ill ? " she exclaimed.

" Not that I know of," he answered. " How extraordinary ! "

" Did you slip ? "

" I—I don't think so."

His pencil-stump was by his boot, but he could not have slipped on that because he had been writing with it. It had not fallen till he had. He stared back at her sheepishly, with little pink flushes on his pale cheeks. He was wearing a well-brushed, shiny blue suit, and his light hair—he had no hat— was not too tidy. He had sold his hat for sixpence, and then lost the sixpence. Scrambling to his feet, he began looking about.

7

" Here it is," said Milly.

She picked up the piece of paper he had dropped and handed it to him. She looked at him hard as she did so.

" If you're not ill," she remarked, " and if you didn't slip, what *I* want to know is what bowled you over ? "

He considered for a moment, then replied:

" It's nice of you to want to know, only if I don't know myself I can't tell you, can I ? "

" It might be worth while trying to find out," she suggested, and suddenly shot a leading question. " Have you had any breakfast ? "

" Ah ! " murmured Simon. " I expect that must be it."

Regaining the pencil-stump from the floor, he completed the operation that had been so surprisingly interrupted, slipped the pencil and paper into a side-pocket, lifted his hand to raise the hat that was not there, and turned towards the door. But her voice detained him.

" I say ! "

" Yes ? "

" I'm going to be abominably rude, but would you like to do a stranger a favour ? "

" If I can, certainly."

" Then promise her that the first thing you'll do after leaving this place is to have a cup of coffee ! "

There were two reasons against making the promise, but he only mentioned one of them. The other was that if he had died as a result of his tumble, his estate would have been valued at one penny.

" No time, I'm afraid," he said. " You see, I've —there's a good chance here, and I mustn't miss it."

" Down on your luck ? "

" Well, I wouldn't put it like that."

" But you need that good chance ? "

" Well, I expect I could do with it."

" You'll miss it if you flop over again in the middle of the interview," she retorted, sagaciously, " and you won't get any sympathy. They'll think it a stunt. Really, you do look as if you needed something inside you. Do be wise ! "

She spoke with a frankness which, he learned later, was characteristic of her, and also with a disarming friendliness. If she was abominably rude, he found it a very pleasant rudeness. Simon Smith was not overburdened with friends.

" Thank you. I will," he lied. " Thank you very much."

Raising his hand again to his absent headgear, he departed somewhat hastily.

He went down the stone, echoing stairs of the public library—Milly listened to the echoes—and out into the street, and along the pavement. The street did not welcome him; it did not even notice him; and the pavement felt rather hard under his feet. But he had a pleasant little memory to walk along with, and that, he decided, was better than coffee. Still, he felt rather guilty as he passed a restaurant —honesty was one of his troubles, and he didn't like even white lies—and when he passed a second he averted his head, pretending not to notice it. He also pretended not to notice a tempting bus. The address to which he was going was only half a mile away, but half a mile to Simon Smith was a considerable distance.

" Silly of me bowling over like that," he told himself. " I must see I don't make an ass of myself again ! "

A few moments later he felt a light touch on his shoulder.

" What about that coffee ? " came a familiar voice.

He turned, startled.

" You've passed three restaurants, you know ! " said Milly.

" Have I ? " he jerked.

" There's one just behind us."

" Ah ! "

He was trying to keep his end up, and she knew all about it. The behaviour of his shiny back had told its story. To spare him the humiliation of voicing a patent truth, she went on:

" Look here, I'm just going to have a cup of coffee myself. What about joining me ? Or— would that hurt ? If things are like I'm guessing they are, you can pay me back when you get that job."

" Suppose I don't get it ? " he asked.

" You're going to get it. After a cup of coffee."

" How will I find you again ? "

" We can fix that."

He gave way. He needed the coffee, but that was not what beat him. It was her insistent friendliness, and the fact that she had shown the interest and taken the trouble to follow him. He could not quite understand it.

Three minutes later they were seated at a small table, the coffee before them, and a large plate of bread and butter added. At first they sat in silence, while the simple meal did its work, and during this silence they tried to " place " each other. Simon's eyes were blue, his expression mild, his stature just under average. What did these things convey, he wondered, to the very live mind behind her own eyes ? Did she read him as a failure, doomed always to hover on the fringe of things, or as a man who, though of limited capacity, might with a little luck rise one day to a small suburban house, and a little garden with a fence all round it, and half a dozen rose trees, and plenty of nasturtiums—they made a good show in the autumn—and the 8.27 every morning ? . . . Milly's eyes were brown, like her name.

Abruptly she broke the silence.

" You told me a beautiful fib in the library, didn't you ? " she remarked, with a bluntness he was already growing to expect from her. " You said you weren't down on your luck ! "

" No, I said I wouldn't put it like that," he corrected her.

" Well, quite a lot would. Perhaps you don't believe in the word ? "

" I think it's a dangerous word."

" I see you've worked it out."

" No, not particularly. But what I mean is that I expect we really get the luck we deserve."

She looked thoughtful.

" I'm out of work, like you," she said, and added quickly, " But don't let that worry you about the coffee—I've got five pounds eight and threepence, and anyway you're going to pay me back. Well, do I deserve to be ? "

The question, it seemed to Simon, was easily answered. He shook his head.

" I don't expect you'll be out for long," he predicted.

" Oh, and what makes you think that ? "

" You don't seem to be the kind of person who'd have much difficulty."

She smiled. " Would you like to know my difficulty ? "

" What ? "

" My looks."

He stared at her in complete astonishment.

" I—I should have thought your looks would have helped," he stammered. " If I may say so."

" You may say so," she laughed. " But they don't. Not me, anyhow. When I find out how my looks are helping—and you can judge in a jiffy—I grow stubborn and say I'll think about it ! I may be an idiot, but—well, that's how I'm made."

" It seems to me a nice way to be made," responded Simon, after a short pause.

" Thank you," answered Milly ; " but the difficulty remains. Only yesterday I turned down a post—chauffeur-secretary—because a man who knew nothing whatever about my qualifications told me I could name my salary. Fat, fast and fifty. Not my style ! Of course, I really ought to have taken the job and driven him into a ditch ! " She became practical, and switched from herself back to him. " Time to be going ? "

" I expect it is," he replied, fighting depression at the idea.

" Well, I mustn't keep you," she said. " Good luck ! "

He got up from his chair and then remembered something.

" How am I going to pay my debt ? " he asked. " We've not arranged that yet." Misinterpreting a sudden little frown, he added rather hastily, " If you let me have your address I could post the amount to you—it wouldn't be necessary to call."

" The amount would be fivepence in stamps," she answered, " and I don't suppose it would kill me if you did call. But I wasn't thinking of that. I can give you my name—Milly Brown—by the way, what's yours ? "

" Simon Smith."

" Thank you. But I can't give you my address. You see, I'm changing it to-day, and I haven't found the new one yet." She did not mention that the new one would have to be cheaper than the old. " That seems to knock my suggestion on the head, doesn't it ? "

" Then may I make one ? " said Simon, displaying bold initiative at last. " Suppose I square the account with a lunch ? That is, if I get the job— which, after all, I don't really expect I will——"

" In that case you *won't* ! " she interrupted. " But if you think you will, then you *might* ! Try that way round for a change, Mr. Smith ! "

There was reproof as well as encouragement in her tone.

" I'll get it," he smiled.

" Good ! Then I'll get my lunch," she responded. " One o'clock ? "

" Yes, here."

He looked vaguely round.

" You didn't have a hat," she reminded him.

" Oh, so I didn't," he answered.

And vanished.

Milly Brown looked after him, and sat at the little table for quite a while after he had gone, in spite of the fact that she should have been searching for a job herself. She was not particularly fond of men, though she was sensible enough to realise their necessity in the scheme of things. She disliked their presumptions and assumptions. But Simon Smith seemed entirely lacking in presumptions and assumptions. In fact, she had never come across any other man quite like him. Let us peep into the private opinion she jotted in her little note-book before leaving the restaurant. She did not ordinarily keep a diary, and this note-book was not a continuous record of events; it was a haphazard collection of odds and ends, reminders, and momentary impressions which would never have existed if the book had not chanced to be one of the fitments of her handbag. Milly hated waste.

" Have just bumped into a most unusual man," ran the entry. " Have given him coffee, and if we're both lucky he's going to give me lunch. But what he needs most is a mother."

CHAPTER TWO

MR. HENRY MILDENHALL

THE ADVERTISEMENT Simon Smith was answering ran, " Man wanted immediately for confidential job, experience unnecessary, honesty essential," and he rang the bell of the small flat to which the advertisement had directed him with more hope than he had felt for many a day. Probably the job had already gone, yet an illogical optimism stirred him. When he had got up that morning and had wended his way breakfastless to the public library, his soul had been depressed and stagnant, but now a new determination was taking the dullness out of his eye and the numbness out of his brain. He cleared his throat softly while he waited—one's voice was apt to be husky if it did not get a good start—brushed a bit of dust from his shiny sleeve, and quickly combed his hair with his fingers.

For these things, he felt, Milly Brown was directly responsible. Perhaps he was a little unfair to himself in awarding her all the credit. Still, her words had undoubtedly warmed his spirit, and he had to justify that luncheon appointment.

The door opened. An elderly, grey-haired man peered out at him. The man had an odd, nervous manner, and his face as he opened the door wore a worried frown. It also looked exceedingly tired. But the next instant it brightened, and Simon received a surprising impression that he was being welcomed.

" Yes—come in, come in ! " exclaimed the man, seizing his arm. " You look exactly—come in ! "

The applicant was pulled into the hall. The advertiser closed the front door and then came round for a closer scrutiny of his visitor. For a few moments neither spoke. Then came the sudden sharp question:

" You have come, of course, in answer to the advertisement ? "

" Yes, sir," replied Simon.

" Well, let us talk. I am Henry Mildenhall. You have heard of me ? No, I see by your expression that you have not. I am a scientist. An inventor. Never mind. This way."

He shoved a door open, and Simon entered a rather untidy sitting-room.

" Sit down."

Simon sat down.

" Now, then. Let us begin ! " But the beginning was delayed while Mr. Mildenhall crossed suddenly to a decanter. " You'll take something ? "

" Thank you, sir, but I don't drink," answered Simon, hoping that by this statement he would earn a good mark.

It was a true statement. Drink went immediately to his head.

" Well, it is not one of my own usual habits," remarked Mr. Mildenhall, offering an unnecessary explanation while he filled his glass, " but I have been overworking lately. Overworking. Yes, and then it has been tiring seeing all these applicants— you are by no means the first. A procession——" The bell rang. " There's another ! "

He darted from the room. Alone, Simon glanced curiously around and about. His eyes paused at a large photograph in a silver frame on a desk. It was a photograph of a very lovely girl in evening-dress. Many would have called her lovelier than Milly Brown, but Simon did not. He was puzzled by something familiar about the features. " But how *can* they be familiar ? " he asked himself. The question was answered in startling fashion several days later.

Mr. Mildenhall returned as abruptly as he had departed. He had been absent for less than a minute. Simon concluded, wrongly, that Mr. Mildenhall had asked the next applicant to wait. He would have been astonished to learn that the applicant had been sent away, and that a notice was now pinned on the door :

" Post filled."

" I hope that will be the last interruption," said the inventor, as he returned. " Now, then, once more ! What was your last job, and why did you lose it ? "

" It was with Dench and Dench, the advertisers," replied Simon. " I lost it—well—when I lost my health."

" I see. Your health is poor ? "

" Not now, sir. It was then, yes."

" H'm ! Well. And that was the only reason ? Not incompetence, by any chance ? You can be quite frank. It won't hurt you."

Simon coloured slightly. He tried not to feel bewildered. Was he being invited to admit incompetence without prejudice ?

" They were cutting down the staff," he temporised. " Perhaps I should have mentioned that first. I—I took it I was one of the least essential.

R.N.S. B

That may have been partly due to the state of my health at the time."

Mr. Mildenhall smiled very faintly. The smile would have been less faint had he been in the humour for it.

" Well, that does not worry me, Mr.—— ? "

" Smith. Simon Smith."

" What would worry me, Mr. Smith, would be to hear that you had been discharged for—say— dishonesty. Betraying confidence——"

" Indeed not, sir ! " exclaimed Simon. He added, with a touch of dignity, " That is one thing, sir, that cannot be said of me. Still, of course, you can satisfy yourself on that point by applying to Messrs. Dench and Dench."

Mr. Mildenhall looked at the applicant hard, then nodded.

" I do not think I shall find that necessary. How long ago did you leave them ? "

" Four months."

" And you have had no job since ? "

" No, sir."

" Honesty, alone, being hardly a marketable commodity ? "

" Eh ? I—well——"

" You could start working for me at once, then ? "

" Oh, yes. Certainly."

" It would be at once."

Mr. Mildenhall turned to a drawer, and while he unlocked it Simon thought, amazed, " I believe I'm getting the job ! " His prospective employer peered into the drawer for a few seconds, almost as though his final decision lay inside, and then brought out a small tube.

" Tell me, Mr. Smith—have you ever done any commercial travelling ? "

Sorely tempted to lie, Simon refrained. So far he had only lied once, about his present health. His insistence on his honesty must be backed up.

" Never," he replied.

" But you think you could do it, if you had a good article to sell ? "

" I—yes, I feel sure I could. It would interest me very much." A sudden vision of Milly Brown—it was an approving vision—made him add, " I believe I could make a success of it."

The vision of Milly Brown applauded.

" I share your belief," said Mr. Mildenhall, while Simon wondered why on earth he should, " but even if we are both wrong, your honesty will remain, and that is of first importance with me. If I am to give you a trial—a week's trial—you will have to realise that my business—in its present stage—is confidential. Very strictly confidential. Of course, you will have to make public the—er—virtues of the article you will be helping to place on the market, but you will have to know certain details—certain details—actually quite unimportant, mere routine details—which for certain reasons must not be made public. Er—is that clear ? "

" Perfectly clear," answered Simon, although it was not. He did not understand why such emphasis was being laid on the secrecy of unimportant details.

Mr. Mildenhall held up the tube.

" Gum," he said.

" An excellent line, sir," commented Simon.

" You think so ? "

" Undoubtedly, sir. If handled in the right way. And, of course, if the article is of a really high quality. Everybody uses gum."

" Though you have not done any commercial travelling, Mr. Smith, I note already the influence of an advertising firm."

" Thank you, sir."

Mr. Mildenhall unscrewed the cap of the tube and squeezed a little of the gum on to a piece of paper. He explained its virtues with an odd detachment, as though he were reciting a lesson in which he was not greatly interested. But Simon was exceedingly interested, for he felt that, despite his mild boasting, his success depended far more upon the gum's virtues than his own. One of the virtues, if Mr. Mildenhall spoke the truth, was that the gum was more adhesive than any other gum on the market ; another, that a thin layer spread over paper could be allowed to dry, and then licked moist and effective again in a second without detriment to the tongue.

" I think you've got a little gold-mine here ! " exclaimed Simon, enthusiastically.

" That we shall see," answered the inventor. " Now let us talk of details."

Simon's heart bounded. He knew it was a rule not to appear too eager, but he could not help himself.

" Do you mean—have I got the job ? " he asked.

" For a week's trial, yes. Shall we say five pounds a week, plus commission, and another five pounds for expenses ? Salary and expenses in advance ? "

Simon was speechless.

" Now listen to your instructions," continued Mr. Mildenhall. " If they seem a little—unusual—out of the ordinary—you will not worry about that. You will start this afternoon. Two o'clock. You can manage that ? "

Simon nodded.

" You will be provided, of course, with samples and full particulars. You will visit six different towns in the area I have selected for you. I have written the names of the towns, in the order in which you will visit them, on your instructions sheet——"

He took an envelope from his pocket as he spoke. " You will find it all here. You will also find the names of your six hotels. You—er—you will be expected at them, and your room at each hotel has already been booked. Naturally the rooms have not been booked in your name, because I did not know the name of my representative when I booked them. I used the name Grainger, so you have better assume that name for business purposes. Is that clear ? "

" Quite clear," replied Simon. " I am to ask at each hotel for the room booked in the name of Grainger."

" That is correct. For the room booked in the name of Grainger. And remember particularly to visit the towns and the hotels in the order I have given—strictly in that order. Make no alteration whatever in the programme I have arranged for you."

" You can count on that, sir."

" Good. I shall. Next. Commercial travellers— you may know this, even though this is your first experience of being one—they chat together in the evenings at their hotels—fraternise—compare notes. I don't say there is anything wrong in this. Obviously there isn't, provided they converse with discretion and do not give away any trade secrets. Nevertheless, you yourself, Mr. Smith, will fraternise as little as possible. As a matter of fact, you may find that some of the hotels I have chosen will help you in this—some, if not perhaps all." He appeared to flounder for a moment, then became definite again. "Anyway, whether you·meet many brother travellers or not, you will not talk about yourself or your job, and you will satisfy no curiosity. Just go about your business quietly, getting what orders you can from the local tradesmen—your firm, by the way, is Nugum Limited—Nugum Limited—and mixing with others as little as you can."

"Excuse me, sir," interrupted Simon. "Am I not to mention the name of my firm to any one, apart from our customers?"

Mr. Mildenhall did not answer at once. He looked undecided. Then he said:

"No—I don't suppose I mean quite that. You are a commercial traveller—a normal commercial traveller—and naturally you will not want to adopt any attitude to suggest that you are not." He frowned at himself. "I mean—well, you do not want to suggest you are a man of mystery. Well, well, of course not! Why should you? But just be discreet. That is a very different thing, eh? Talk as little as is reasonable."

"I understand what you mean exactly, sir," Simon assured him, without feeling that he really understood at all.

Mr. Mildenhall looked relieved, and continued, "I think you are going to turn out the very man I want, Mr. Smith. I find your attitude satisfactory. And now we come to the—to the part that is particularly confidential. The reason for this is—well——"

He paused for a moment, his indecision returning. He poured himself out another drink.

" Is it necessary for me to know the reason, sir ? " asked Simon, endeavouring to increase his satisfactory qualities. " You are engaging me to carry out your instructions."

" Yes, that is so," responded Mr. Mildenhall, relieved a second time. " And, after all, the instructions are quite simple. I have—of course—other representatives. Other representatives. They attend to other sides of my business. Now, one of these representatives will call on you each evening, at your hotel. Be sure you are in to receive them. No cinemas, I am afraid. You will report the day's doings to them—just verbally, you know—hear anything they have to say—and you will hand them——"

He took a key from his pocket and opened a small black dispatch-box. From the box he extracted a little bundle of fat, heavily-sealed envelopes. Simon wondered whether they had been secured with Nugum. But he wondered even more why Mr. Mildenhall's hand was not steady as he held the bundle up. Was it the whisky ? Mr. Mildenhall himself noticed his unsteadiness, and muttered, " Yes, I am certainly overworking—I must take a rest presently." He laid the bundle on the table.

" You have your own instructions. These—instructions—are to be passed on to the six representatives you will meet. One each night. One to each. You will take the utmost care of them, and always keep them locked in this box which, with the key, will be in your charge when you start. The envelopes, of course, are marked. Be sure to deliver the correct envelope in every case."

Mr. Mildenhall's attitude was undoubtedly strange, and something in his expression at that moment caused Simon uneasiness. He felt a vague chill. He suppressed a curious desire to shiver. He did not know why. . . . of course, it was ridiculous. . . .

" Just a matter of organisation," Mr. Mildenhall was saying. " In fact, a routine experiment. However, that is not your concern. Your concern is to secure orders for the gum, and to—deliver these six envelopes."

As he was about to replace the envelopes in the box, Simon caught sight of the top one.

" Won't I need the names, sir ? The names of the people I am to give them to ? " he asked. " I see you have only written the town."

Mr. Mildenhall turned away for a moment and stared out of the window. If Simon had seen his expression then, his attempt to repress a shiver would have failed.

" Yes, I am coming to that," answered the inventor, turning back. His expression was normal again. " It brings me to my final instruction—last but by no means least, Mr. Smith. In fact, as important as any. My representatives—well, they move about a good deal. They change their districts, and—for that reason, I cannot be quite sure which—that is, in what order—they will call upon you. They will, of course, introduce themselves—give you their names—and after they have gone, each evening after they have gone, you will ring me up here, at my flat, report progress, and mention the names of your visitors. Or, I should say, the name of your visitor, because, of course, there will be only one each night. Er—be very careful about the names, Mr. Smith. Be sure that you get them accurately and completely."

" I shall see there is no mistake," replied Simon.

" And I am certain I can count on you. Yet— though this may appear to contradict what I have just said—I am going to ask one more favour of you. Have you any objection to taking an oath ? "

" An oath, sir ? "

" Yes. Quite a simple one. I would like you to swear that, whatever happens—whatever happens— you will keep this matter secret. I refer, of course, to the particular arrangements and details."

For the first and only time, Simon Smith hesitated. He was of course fully determined to stick to his word, and an oath always vaguely worried him. It was, as Mr. Mildenhall himself had implied, a contradiction of normal confidence, and lifted a comfortable, earthly trust to embarrassing celestial regions. Mr. Mildenhall noticed the hesitation, though it was only momentary, and added quickly, with rather pathetic anxiety :

" Just for the week, you know—only for the week."

" Yes, sir, of course, I'll swear it," Simon then answered. " I swear."

The breath which Mr. Mildenhall had been holding escaped with a little swish.

" Thank you. Well, I think that is all, for the time being. Oh, no. Your money. I will give it to you now—as a sign that my confidence in you is complete."

He produced the money—ten crisp pound notes. Simon accepted them with a little flush. The very feel of them seemed to lay the world at his feet.

" I—I assure you, sir," he stammered, as he got

up from his chair, " I greatly appreciate your trust. And that oath was not really necessary. I should not have betrayed the trust in any case."

Impressed with his new employee's sincerity, Mr. Mildenhall looked at him with a new expression. It was a little moment to which Simon's mind subsequently reverted, and which he never forgot.

" That is good to hear, Mr. Smith," said the inventor. " That is very good to hear. I rely on you. And I thank you."

He conducted him to the door and opened it.

" Two o'clock, then, Mr. Smith. Or perhaps I should now say, Mr. Grainger ? Two o'clock. Your car will be outside here, with everything in it. I did ask you whether you could drive, did I not ? That, of course, is essential. Upon my soul, there have been so many applicants that . . . Well, two o'clock."

He shoved Simon out. As the door closed, Simon stood, stunned. He had never driven a car in his life.

On the other side of the door Henry Mildenhall, discovering a sudden dampness on his forehead, took out his pocket handkerchief and mopped.

CHAPTER THREE

JOURNEY'S BEGINNING

FOR a few moments, as Simon stood outside the door, a world that had turned miraculously to gold became black again. Four months of desperate searching had, at last, brought him to a job, and ten pound notes were in his pocket. Now, because he could not drive a car, he would have to relinquish both. To be able to drive a car, Mr. Mildenhall had said, was essential, and his plans were so exact, and so insisted on, that the idea of any re-arrangement did not enter Simon's mind. He turned back to the door miserably, and saw the notice, " Post filled," which had not been removed. He would have to ring now, and have it taken away.

But as his finger moved reluctantly towards the bell, something flashed into his mind, flashed like a ray of sunlight bursting unexpectedly through dark clouds. It came with a vision of Milly Brown's disappointed face. The lips were moving, repeating a remark she had made to him over their coffee, and reminding him of it : " Only yesterday I turned down a post—chauffeur-secretary——"

His finger paused as it touched the bell.

" No—but that would be impossible ! " his thoughts gasped.

He imagined her replying, with the philosophy she had begun to teach him, " Think it's impossible, and it will be—think it isn't, and it may not be ! "

The philosophy hit him now like a sledge-hammer.

It hit him away from the bell he had been about to press, and out into the road. With his mind in a whirl, he walked back to the restaurant. His mind was still in a whirl when he got there.

A clock across the road struck midday. He had an hour to wait, and that hour was one of the worst he had ever endured. He was haunted by doubts and questions; the doubts were concerning himself, the questions were concerning Milly Brown. Was he an idiot ? Was he worse than an idiot ? Was he being unfair, and should he return to Mr. Mildenhall and tell him the truth ? Suppose Milly did not come ? Even if she did come, she might already have got a job. What then ? Or if she had not got a job, she might not accept the mad one he was about to offer. And what *then* ? And even if she accepted it, how could it be worked ?

His agony was ended at three minutes to one. Standing outside the restaurant, he suddenly picked Milly's neat figure out of a little approaching tide of people. The luncheon hour was filling the pavements. In a few seconds she was up to him, and stopped while the tide flowed on.

" Never mind," she said, after a quick study of his expression. " I've drawn a blank, too."

His next expression was not so easy to read, for all her intelligence. Delight mingled with his sympathy. The theory that he was selfishly glad she had shared his bad luck did not even occur to her.

" I—I'm not sure that I've drawn a blank," he stammered.

" Oh, well done ! "

" No, wait a moment. You see——" He paused, then blurted out, " It's going to depend on *you* ! "

" On me ? " She looked astonished. " How can *I* help ? "

" Let's stroll for a few minutes."

" Why not talk inside ? "

But he shook his head. He had either ten pounds or a penny in his pocket, and he could not treat her to lunch till he knew which. For he had decided one thing quite definitely. If he were forced to turn the job down, Mr. Mildenhall must have his money back intact, without deductions. . . . Yes, but if he turned the job down, could Mr. Mildenhall replace him by two o'clock ? In an hour ? He ought to have gone back at once ! He wasn't being fair. . . .

She saw his mind working desperately, took his arm, and led him up a side street.

" Now tell me," she said.

The difficulty was, there were things he could not tell.

" Well—the position's rather extraordinary," he began. " In fact, I don't really understand it myself—all the details, I mean——"

" Perhaps I can help you with the details," she interposed. " I have been described in one reference as ' able and intelligent '—though I'm not sure whether I am, really ! "

" Yes, but that's one of the extraordinary parts of it—I mustn't talk about the details." She looked at him sharply. " Oh, it's all quite respectable," he assured her, hastily. " At least—yes, of course it is. I liked the chap I saw immensely, even though he was a bit of a mystery. But—well——"

" Courage ! " she smiled. " What's the position, without the details ? "

" Commercial traveller. A week's trial. I'm

supposed to start at two—in an hour—by myself in a car, and I can't drive."

" Well, that's certainly awkward," she admitted. " Why didn't you tell him you couldn't drive ? "

" Because the car wasn't mentioned till the very end, just as he was showing me out," replied Simon. " I think he thought he'd mentioned it. He'd seen lots of other applicants, and probably imagined he'd told me like the rest. The whole thing was fixed up. Why, he even gave me my salary and expenses in advance. The money's in my pocket at this moment."

He paused, and she anticipated his next information.

" And you didn't go back because you suddenly thought of me ? "

" Yes. You mentioned you'd applied for a chauffeur's job."

" I remember. But you can't afford to run a chauffeur ! "

" He gave me enough for two." He glanced at her anxiously.   " Mad, eh ? "

" Bats ! " she answered. " Let's have lunch and talk about it."

His heart leapt. "Wait a moment, wait a moment!" he exclaimed, as she turned. " You see, I—I can only give you that lunch if I take the job ! "

" In that case, I expect you'll have to take the job," she retorted. " Anyway, Mr. Smith, I'm hungry, if you're not, and I can't make important decisions on an empty stomach ! "

She seized his arm and switched him round. He laughed. It was the first time he had laughed for quite a while.

Over lunch he gave her as full an account as was possible without breaking his vow of the strange interview with Henry Mildenhall. She listened intently, thought the gum sounded good, and the salary better. "How much is the commission?" she asked. He admitted that he did not know. "What is the gum selling at?" came her next question. He admitted he did not know that, either, but added that all those details, assumedly, would be on his instructions sheet.

"You haven't got that yet?"

"No. I expect it will be in the car, with the samples."

Milly lowered her eyes to the tablecloth, stared fixedly at a crust of bread without seeing it, and then raised her eyes again.

"Did he ask for any references?" she inquired.

"No," replied Simon.

"Did you think that funny?"

"That anyone should trust my face? Yes, very funny."

She smiled. "Well, I seem to be doing the same thing, don't I? But then I've known you an hour longer than Mr. Mildenhall has. What beats me is that *anybody's* face should be trusted in a job that seems to be rather confidential." Then she shot the direct question towards which the others had been leading. "Do you think this is anything shady?"

Simon considered for several seconds before replying. He realised the importance of the question. It was important to Milly as well as to him.

"No, I don't," he answered at last.

His voice was definite. Milly nodded. Simon felt

that her practical attitude would be as big an asset in the adventure as her capacity to drive a car.

" I expect you're right," she said, " but I'd like to know what makes you so certain, if you could tell me ? "

" Yes, I can tell you," responded Simon. " If he trusted my face, I trusted his."

" Perhaps he's a better judge of a face ? "

" Or a worse." A sudden uneasiness assailed him. " But, look here, I'm not going to risk dragging you into any trouble——"

" Don't worry, Mr. Smith. There probably won't be any trouble—and if there is, well, two can meet it as well as one. I'm accepting the job, provided we can agree on salary."

" We'll go halves ! " he exclaimed.

" Sorry ! Nothing doing." She laughed at his blank expression. " You meant half the ten pounds, didn't you ? "

" Of course."

" I thought so. But I'll only take half the five. I can manage on that beautifully—and, don't forget, you've got to stand the petrol."

They wrangled a while over this, but she was adamant, and he gave way. Then they came to the chief difficulty. How were they going to arrange their own details ? Simon had already implied his firm disbelief that Mr. Mildenhall would approve of a chauffeur.

This, indeed, was a spiritual as well as a practical snag, and it was the only thing that worried Simon. He eased his conscience with the reflection that, distasteful though deception was, the present deception would not be practised against his employer's interest, but should actually benefit him in the long run. Mr. Mildenhall had unconsciously placed himself in a dilemma by mentioning the confidential details before completing the qualifications necessary for carrying them out. The new employee, in a situation not of his own making, was using his judgment as to the best method of dealing with it.

While Simon struggled, not perhaps with complete success, over the moral aspect of the case, Milly wrestled with the practical. The problem was that the car would assumedly be outside Mr. Mildenhall's flat, and that Mr. Mildenhall would assumedly watch his employee depart. " And I don't even know how to start the thing," Simon confessed, with shame. It was over her last spoonful of rice pudding that Milly got her brain-wave.

" Is there a telephone near the flat ? " she asked.

Simon recalled that there was. He had noticed a public booth at the corner.

" Is it within sight of the front door ? "

" Yes."

" Then we're saved, Mr. Smith ! " she exclaimed.

He listened to her plan with respectful awe.

Promptly at two, Simon Smith presented himself at his employer's, to find Mr. Mildenhall already standing on the pavement beside the car. It was a small saloon, dark blue and very neat in appearance, and the back seat was piled with two cases and a box. The box Simon recognised. It was the black dispatch-box in which were the six heavily-sealed envelopes.

Greeting Simon with evident relief, and handing him his instructions sheet, Mr. Mildenhall gave his final orders, to which Simon attended carefully.

The new employee prolonged the interview with questions, for he was also attending covertly to the telephone-booth at the corner. He noticed a girl enter the booth, and the girl noticed him, though neither gave any sign of recognition. Mr. Mildenhall wished his new employee luck. The new employee took his place in the driver's seat. While Simon fumbled, the girl in the telephone-booth dialled her number.

Mr. Mildenhall raised his head.

" Is that my telephone ringing ? " he exclaimed, glancing up towards his open window.

" Yes, sir—I think it's been ringing for some time," answered Simon, his heart thumping. "Please don't wait, sir. Everything's in order, and I shall get right off—and phone you up to-night, as arranged."

The bell went on ringing. Mr. Mildenhall nodded and ran indoors. But the moment he was out of sight, Milly ran faster from the telephone-booth. Simon slid into the next seat as she dived into the car, and a moment later they had started their strange journey with a violent jerk. . . .

Mr. Mildenhall replaced the receiver with a puzzled frown. The person who was calling him appeared to have given up suddenly. He glanced out of the window at the empty street. He sat down, feeling suddenly faint and sick.

CHAPTER FOUR

ROOM NUMBER SIX

THE FIRST of the six towns was Brackham, but they did not discover this till they had travelled a mile in the wrong direction. Then Milly stopped the car, somewhat breathlessly, and asked whether it would not be a good idea to know where they were going.

" I expect that is fairly necessary," replied Simon, equally breathless. Milly's driving had not been pacific, and, in spite of his ethical gymnastics, he felt rather like a small boy running away from a farmer and his dog. Not anxious to add a policeman to the chase, he inquired, " I suppose it's all right to stop in the middle of the road ? "

" Those people behind us don't seem to think so," answered Milly, and drove on to a more reasonable spot.

Here they stopped again, and Simon consulted his instructions.

" Our first place is Brackham, Hertfordshire," he said. He did not mention that their first hotel was the King's Head. That raised a point that could be discussed later.

" North—it *would* be," commented Milly, " as we're heading south ! What part of Hertfordshire ? "

" I don't know," he responded.

" Well, as I don't, either," she returned, " I think your first business expense, Mr. Smith, will have to be a map ! "

A bookshop was within sight. A shilling map informed them that Brackham was between thirty and thirty-five miles away. The distance was satisfactory.

" Get ready for shocks," warned Milly. " I'm going to tread on it, so you'll have all the time you can before the shops close ! "

Unfortunately, however, there was small opportunity to tread on it for many built-up miles. London, with its irritating traffic lights and traffic policemen, extended far along their route, and it seemed to Simon that they were never going to shake themselves out of the endless dreary streets. Out of the corner of his eye he watched his companion with, perhaps, too much admiration. Thousands of others were manipulating cars with equal skill, accelerating, slackening, changing gears, gliding through spaces that looked too narrow to hold them, obeying subconsciously the rule of the road; but these others were merely doing what was expected of them. The same coolness and efficiency in Milly bore the magic of a miracle.

Houses grew less. Space grew more. At last they reached open country, and Milly stepped on it. Rather anxiously Simon watched the needle move from twenty-five to thirty, from thirty to forty, from forty to fifty. He hoped it would have no further ambition, but the hope was disappointed. It went to fifty-five. " I say, aren't we going at a pace ? " he murmured. " Yes," answered Milly, as the needle touched fifty-seven. After that he decided not to talk.

They entered Brackham's outskirts at half-past three.

Brackham proved to be a small town, and Simon wondered why Mr. Mildenhall had chosen it. It was dull and uninspiring, as well as small, with depressing grey streets and little outward indication of the life it lived beneath its surface. Simon was oversensitive to first impressions, and his first impression of Brackham filled him with uncomfortable forebodings. The forebodings were vague and nameless, but the disturbing elements of his queer interview with Mr. Mildenhall seemed to brood over the place like a cloud.

He wondered how he would have felt had he entered Brackham without the encouragement of a companion. The companion, though her mood remained cheerful, was equally unimpressed.

" One night in a hole like this will be just enough ! " she commented. " And from the look of the shopping district, Mr. Smith, I don't believe you're going to need more ! "

" No—I don't think we shall find many shops interested in gum here," he agreed.

" What do you do ? Just go from shop to shop and see what happens ? "

" I expect that's the idea."

" Or do you want to find an hotel first ? That doesn't look a bad one, over there on the right——"

" No, I won't worry about an hotel just yet," he interrupted quickly. The hotel she indicated displayed a blue stag ; the one he had to look out for would display, he assumed, the head of a king. " Ah ! There's a stationer just beyond ! Would you stop there, please ? "

He had studied his samples during the journey, before the increasing pace had caused him merely to study their chances of survival. The gum had been put up in various forms, shapes and sizes, and the two bags contained examples of each variety. When Milly pulled up at the kerb he seized a bag and alighted nervously. Then, pausing to take a deep breath—he did not hear Milly's " Go in and win ! "—he entered the shop in a panic.

A sharp-visaged woman eyed him unfavourably.

" Er—could I see the manager ? " he stammered.

" You are seeing the manager," replied the woman.

" Oh ! Well, good-afternoon. Might I show you—— ? "

" No, you mightn't. I'm not buying anything. Good-afternoon."

He emerged with a face like a sunset.

" No luck ? " smiled Milly.

" Not that time," he murmured.

" Well, there'll be plenty more times ! Isn't that another stationer's across the road ? Try that ! "

He nodded, and crossed the road. His second interview was conducted with a very old man, and he varied his opening remark.

" Are you the manager ? " he asked.

" Eh ? " piped the old man.

" The manager," repeated Simon.

" Oh, what about him ? " inquired the old man.

" Can I see him ? "

" I wouldn't advise it. He's got measles."

At the third shop Arthur decided to ignore the management altogether. Placing his bag on the counter, he opened it to let the contents speak for themselves before he ruined the conversation.

The shopman peered in, then came round the counter and led his visitor to a shelf.

" Gum," he said, pointing to a row of bottles.
He led him to another shelf.

" More gum," he said.

He led him to a drawer and opened it.

" More gum," he said.

But this time Simon made an effort, realising that
he must not take every situation sitting.

" Do you know why you've got so much gum ? "
he demanded.

" I dare say I could tell you," replied the shopman,
" but I'm always ready to learn."

" It's because one can never sell an inferior article.
You'd find mine better."

The shopman smiled.

" You fellers know how to talk," he conceded,
" but sometimes we know how to talk better. Now
answer this. If your gum isn't better than what I've
got, how shall I sell it ? And if it is, how shall I sell
what I've got ? "

Simon couldn't find the answer, and the shopman
told him to call again next Christmas, but although
he had drawn another blank he felt he had made some
progress. He had been informed that he knew how to
talk !

Rejoining Milly—he had only known her half a
dozen hours, yet already she gave him a sense of
home—he described the interview and received her
congratulations.

" You'll be all right, once you've found your feet,"
she declared confidently. " Goodness, how can you
expect to get orders right away—before you've
gained any experience, and in a dead-and-alive hole
like this, too ? "

" Of course, you'd cheer anybody."

" Well, that's a game for two players."

His manner improved still further at the next shop, though it produced no practical results, and by six o'clock, with Brackham completely combed, he was still waiting for his first order.

" Well, that's that," pronounced Milly, " and now, I suppose, we look for our hotel. Do we go to the same one, or do we think of Mrs. Grundy ? "

" Yes—we've got to consider that, haven't we ? " replied Simon.

What he had to consider was the expected evening visitor, and the fact that the visit, he supposed, had to be kept even from Milly. Could the secret be kept if they were at the same hotel ? But the idea of parting from Milly, even for the night, was a cheerless and lonely one.

" Separate hotels," she said, noting his hesitation.

" Yes, I—I think that might be best," he answered, and added hastily, " Not because I want it, of course."

" Of course," she smiled. " I know that isn't the reason. And the reason isn't really Mrs. Grundy, either, is it ? "

" Well—no."

She nodded.

" Of course not ! That defunct lady was just my joke. Listen, Mr. Smith, I'm going to say something. I know you've got a problem—I mean, a problem that's quite separate from that of making people buy gum. I'm not going to add to it by being curious, or by troubling you more with my presence than is necessary. But if you get into a jam I won't like it any better than I expect you'd like it if I got into one. We'd want to help each other, wouldn't we ?

So let's remember that—both of us. I shall put up at the Blue Stag, and if it's not breaking your solemn oath to let me know where you propose staying, I'll turn up in the morning with the car, at whatever time you decide."

" You're the most understanding person I've ever met," answered Simon. " I don't know how you do it ! There wouldn't be any harm, of course, if we had a bit of dinner together——"

But she interrupted him with a shake of her head.

" No, we won't do that. Business is over for the day——"

" That wouldn't be business."

" Well, perhaps I should have said *my* business. You may have some still to come, for all I know, and I don't want you to feel you have to be social." He frowned. " You know—filling in books with all the sales you haven't made," she smiled. " Well, what time to-morrow ? Better make it early. " Nine ? "

" Yes, nine will do."

" And which hotel ? The King's Head ? "

" How did you know ? " he asked, astonished.

" You just couldn't keep your eyes off it when we drove past," she laughed, " though personally I couldn't see the attraction ! Well, it's just round the corner."

Of all the dismal buildings in Brackham, the King's Head Hotel was surely the most dismal. Its perfectly flat exterior was unrelieved by bay window, balcony, or architectural protuberance of any kind, and even the grime of years had been flattened into its surface. You only knew it was an hotel because it said so in peeling letters over the open front door.

If it possessed a back door, you apparently had to go right round the block to find it, for the hotel was joined on to other flat buildings on either side without any indication where the hotel ended and the other buildings began.

" Shall I wait here till you report O.K. ? " asked Milly, as she stopped the car.

" Yes, please," answered Simon. He assumed that everything would be O.K., but the arrangement delayed her departure.

He entered the dim, cold space that called itself the lobby. There was a counter on the left, inadequately illuminated by an economical gas-jet, and there was a man behind the counter. He was entering figures in a large ledger, and he looked up mechanically as Simon approached.

" If you want a room, try the Crown," said the man. " We're full up."

" But my room's booked," replied Simon. " At least, so I understand."

" Oh, booked ! What name ? "

" Smi—Grainger."

" Grainger. Grainger." He referred to a sheet. " Ah, yes. Grainger, Room No. 6." Thus, casually, Simon first heard a room number he was to dream of. " Show this gentleman up, Bob. And tell Jane No. 5's ringing."

" Wait a minute ! " exclaimed Simon. " I've got some things outside."

" Car ? "

" Er—in a car, yes."

" Then you'll want the garage——"

" No, it's being garaged somewhere else. Just the things."

" I see. Help the gentleman with his luggage, Bob, and then take him up to No. 6. Hey! Jane! Hurry, No. 5's been ringing for ten minutes! "

While a slow-motion maid went to answer a bell that had been ringing for ten minutes, a boy with an unclean face preceded Simon into the street. The boy seemed vaguely surprised to find an attractive young lady in the car, but the attractive young lady promptly stopped his staring and directed his attention to the bags and the box at the back. The boy took the bags, but Simon forestalled him with the box. That was too valuable to entrust to anybody else! Simon also took a parcel containing a few necessary purchases—including pyjamas and a toothbrush—he had made in the town.

" Well—until nine to-morrow," said Milly. " Good-night."

" Good-night," answered Simon.

He watched her drive away, and then followed the boy back into the hotel.

He was conducted up a flight of steps that had lost whatever glory they may once have possessed, and then along a short passage, to Room No. 6. The boy opened the door with a key, deposited the bags on a luggage-rack at the foot of the bed, paused vaguely for a possible tip that did not materialise, and then left the room, closing the door behind him.

Alone, Simon sat down for a few moments to collect his thoughts, and to fight the inevitable reaction that had set in. He seemed to have entered a gloomy peace after a day of rush and bustle that had led him to strange action, confused thinking and conflicting emotions. The one definite and pleasant

issue was that it had led to Milly Brown. But unfortunately Milly Brown was not by his side to
cheer him at this moment.

His eyes roamed round the room, taking in its
details. It was a large room. He felt rather small in
it. A little, cosy apartment would have suited his
humour better. Just as he felt small in the room, his
parcel looked small on the bed—as inadequate to
face the situation as himself. The parcel contained
all his worldly belongings, apart from the clothes
and pockets he stood up in, and a bed of this size
must disdain such insignificance ! The contemptu-
ous bed protruded from the centre of the right-hand
wall. An octagonal table with a red cover was near
the luggage-rack at its foot. On the table was the
black dispatch-box. The dispatch-box was not big,
but in some queer way it seemed to dwarf everything else, and to bear a significance even greater
than the room's dimensions. The fireplace, its
bareness concealed by a cheap green screen featuring
an impossible elephant, was in the wall opposite the
bed, the space between covered by a faded rug.
Lying in bed you would look over the low ridge of
your feet at the elephant, unless, disliking the sight,
you raised your eyes higher and looked at your own
reflection mirrored above the dark marbled mantelpiece. Your reflection, if it truly reflected your
mood, might not be an improvement on the elephant,
and in Simon's case it would be just as impossible.
For what would he, Simon Smith, be doing here in
this vast bed, with unearned pounds in his neatly-
folded trousers, with a job beyond his capacity, and
a mind set on fire by a girl even more beyond him
then the job ?

Beside the bed was the chair that would receive the neatly-folded trousers ; on the other side, a little wicker table, with a candlestick on it. A red candlestick, to match the red tablecloth, but not the green elephant. The elephant did not match anything. Washstand, left of fireplace. Chest-of-drawers, by the door. Why was he noting all these details ? He did not know. Surely he would never want to recall this room that gave him such a queer cold feeling ? Hanging cupboard—wardrobe, rather (he never liked the expression hanging cupboard) —wardrobe ? Where was a wardrobe ? No wardrobe. Unless that door on the right of the green elephant was a cupboard with hooks ? Yes, probably. But what on earth did it matter ? He had nothing to hang in a wardrobe !

Window, opposite the door. What was the outlook ? He got up and walked to the window. The outlook was a water-pipe and a wall.

He turned as someone knocked on the door. It was the slow-motion maid. She had a sort of heavy attractiveness. Just enough to interest, without extending, tired business men at the end of a weary day. Some of the tired business men called her " Kiss-me-quick." Kissing was the only thing she could do in a hurry.

" Will you be taking dinner ? " she asked.

" Yes," he answered. " What time is it ? "

" Any time, sir. It's on now."

" Thank you. I'll go down."

She stood in the doorway, sizing him up. Life was very dull in Brackham.

" I can do your room while you're gone," she said.

" Yes. After I've had a wash," he replied.

" I've not put out the towels, but there's a clean towel in the bathroom across the passage."

" Is there ? Thank you."

The practical, unilluminating conversation over, she remained in the doorway while he passed her. It was a little trick of hers, and it often came off. But even if Milly had not filled Simon's mind, he would not have been interested, and her vague smile faded as he left the room untempted by momentary proximity. She entered the room gloomily. Suddenly the smile returned. He was hurrying back.

" Forgotten something ? " she inquired, archly.

" Yes," he said.

He seized the dispatch-box, put it in a drawer, locked the drawer, and pocketed the key. She made a grimace at his back as it vanished for the second time.

Before descending to the dining-room Simon returned once more to the bedroom. The maid was temporarily absent. For some reason he could not explain, his eyes roamed towards the cupboard, and he went to it and opened it. He had to turn a key to do. so. The cupboard, to his relief, was empty. . . . Well, of course it was empty ! What had he expected ?

Annoyed with himself, and hearing the maid in the passage, he quickly closed the cupboard door and ran out of the room. His annoyance increased when he ran into the maid and nearly caused her to drop a towel. " Aren't you in a hurry ? " she exclaimed. As he descended the stairs, now at a more dignified gait, he caught a vague glimpse of a man who had just entered the hotel from the street, and was crossing to the counter. Rather tall, and with a black moustache. " I wonder if my visitor will be anything like that ? " he thought. " But I don't suppose he'll turn up till later."

Still, he hurried his meal, or attempted to—the service was disconcertingly slow—and he discouraged the conversation of a brother-commercial who called him " Laddie " three times and then gave up. Normally, Simon would have enjoyed a chat, but recalling Mr. Mildenhall's instructions, he decided to take no risks.

Just as he was finishing the meal, the omnipresent maid appeared in the doorway and beckoned to him. He left his chair immediately.

" There's someone to see you, in your room," she said.

" In my room ? " he exclaimed.

" He asked to go right up—said you were expecting him, and not to disturb you till you'd finished. He's been here half an hour."

Simon thanked her, and ascended the stairs with a thumping heart.

CHAPTER FIVE

THE FIRST CALLER

THE VISITOR was sitting on the edge of the bed, smoking. He was not tall, as Simon had imagined he would be, and he did not possess a black moustache. He was of medium height, with the face of a boxer, even to a boxer's nose. He was, in fact, if one could judge by outward appearances, one of the most unpleasant individuals Simon had ever been called upon to interview.

"Don't mind my making myself at home, do you?" he said, as Simon appeared. "No ceremony in our business, you know. Sit down."

"Thank you! I see you are already sitting down," answered Simon, ruffled by this unpropitious opening, and undecided as to what attitude he ought to adopt. It seemed a little unusual to be invited to sit in his own room!

"Come, you didn't expect me to stand while you finished your dinner, did you?" retorted the visitor. "Now let's get down to it, because there's no need to keep you, now you *are* here. Have you had a good day?"

Simon hesitated. The man ran on:

"Well, that's right—you're wise to be cautious. I know who *you* are—you're the gentleman in No. 6 —but I haven't proved to you yet who *I* am, though I shouldn't think that would take much guessing. You're travelling for the firm, aren't you?"

" That is correct," answered Simon. " And—er—
you know the firm, of course ? "

" This it ? "

He put three big fingers into his waistcoat pocket
and produced a tube of gum.

" Quite right," nodded Simon. " Nugum."

" Yes, and you're a new member of the Nugum
staff, ain't you ? " grinned the visitor. " Mr. Mildenhall has his own ideas about staff, and you never
know who he's going to engage next. I expect
you'll come up against some rum 'uns before you've
finished. Even rummer than me, eh ? Well, I put
a question to you—just as a matter of form, you
know, just as a matter of form—and you haven't
answered it. Done any business ? "

Simon had been waiting for his guest to mention
Mildenhall's name. This, coupled with the evidence
of the gum itself, set his doubts at rest, although he
did not love his guest any the more for having
proved his credentials.

" No, so far, I have not done any business,"
admitted the new member of the staff, " but I
haven't had much time yet. Only two hours, to be
exact. But to-morrow I—I hope to begin getting
orders."

" That's the spirit," smiled the visitor. " That's
the way to get on. Never be down-hearted, and
never quarrel. If the shop-people don't love you,
turn the other cheek, and if somebody slaps the other
cheek, then turn back to the first one. I've been in
the game donkeys' years, and I know. Why, see
that ? " He pointed to his nose. " I got that broke
for being too fresh." Suddenly he stared at Simon,
as though a thought had struck him. " Yes, and I

should say *you* could lose your temper—and do
something rash all of a sudden, eh ?—something you
might be sorry for afterwards ! So watch your solar
plexus. . . . Well, there we are. That's about all,
isn't it ? Have you got anything for me ? "

The interview with Mr. Mildenhall had been
strange, but this was even stranger. Had everything been covered already, apart from the handing
over of the envelope ?

" Yes—I have something for you," replied
Simon slowly, " but——"

" No ' buts ' between members of the Nugum
staff," chipped in the visitor.

" No. Quite so. Only, have you nothing more to
ask me ? "

" Not if you haven't any more to tell me."

" Yes. Exactly. But I thought you might have
some message for Mr. Mildenhall ? "

" Oh, did you ? " The visitor paused and
regarded his boots. Large boots, and not as well
cared for as Simon's. " Yes. I see. That's right.
Well, tell him—tell him—you'll be writing to him,
eh ? "

A thought flashed into Simon's mind. He did not
know whether it had any value, and there was no
time to review it. Perhaps—ran the thought—
Simon's comments on his visitors might be of more
interest to Mr. Mildenhall than the visitor's comments on Simon ? He decided not to mention that
his own comments would be conveyed telephonically, within a very few minutes.

" Yes, I shall be writing," lied Simon.

" Good ! If you forget to stamp the letter, make
sure it's worth the double postage." Evidently the

visitor considered this very funny. " Tell him that Leicester's a wash-out, but Nottingham's O.K. As a matter of fact, I think he might start a branch in Nottingham. Tell him I say so."

" Who says so ? " inquired Simon.

" Eh ? " blinked the visitor.

" Won't he want your name ? "

A very odd expression flashed into the visitor's face for an instant. His lips twitched, and all at once Simon wondered whether the unpleasant fellow were as contented and as self-assured as he affected to be.

" Yes—of course—he'll want my name," said the visitor. " Fancy forgetting that ! It's Thomas Raikes. Don't forget. Thomas Raikes. R-a-i-k-e-s. There, now that's the lot. Come on ! Let's finish it ! " He spoke with impatience.

" This chap's worried," thought Simon. " Why didn't I notice it before ? "

Aloud, Simon said, " You mean, you want me to give you your instructions ? "

" Eh ? Yes, instructions, that's it. I've got to know where I'm to go next."

He jumped up from the bed, leaving his impression upon it as a doubtful gift. Simon walked to the drawer in which he had locked the dispatch-box. He walked with a strange reluctance, and Thomas Raikes watched him all the way, with a sort of unpleasant fascination. In fact, he did not remove his eyes from Simon until the first of the six sealed envelopes was in his hand. Then some tension relaxed in him, and he exclaimed :

" Ah ! Thanks ! "

He moved away, and with his back to Simon,

broke the seal. Simon meanwhile replaced the dispatch-box in the drawer, relocked the drawer, and pocketed the key. When he turned, Raikes was pocketing the envelope.

" In order ? " asked Simon.

" Quite in order," answered Raikes. For an instant his eye rested on the drawer. " Yes, quite in order." Suddenly he looked at Simon and leered. " Well, don't forget about that solar plexus of yours. You look mild enough, but it's the mild ones who go off the handle—bing, just like that ! So long ! "

A second later he was gone.

Simon stared at the closed door, trying hard not to feel uneasy. The truth was that he felt desperately uneasy. Yet he had merely carried out his instructions.

Why had Thomas Raikes conducted the interview in that queer spirit ? Was he the kind of man in whom Mr. Mildenhall, so keen on honesty, would place his trust ? Why had he turned his back while opening the envelope ? And why had he referred, on two separate occasions, to Simon's solar plexus ?

" I've never gone off the handle in my life ! " reflected Simon. " What the dickens did he mean ? "

He turned towards the bed, regarded the impression of his visitor's recent presence, and went to it and smoothed it away. He wished he could have eliminated its originator as easily from his mind.

" Well, now for Mr. Mildenhall," he murmured.

He left his room, descended the stairs to the depressing lobby, and found the hotel telephone-booth. He spent half an hour trying to get on to Mr. Mildenhall. There was no reply.

CHAPTER SIX

NIGHT DISTURBANCES

IF BRACKHAM was depressing in the day-time, it was doubly so at night. Apart from its public houses, where tired or bored folk attempted to forget the monotony of existence in local liquor or darts, the sole entertainment was a small cinema with its entrance up a side street. True, the entrance was brilliantly illuminated. As Milly Brown passed beneath a strange glass roof thrust out from the building as an enticement to glamour, her complexion became momentarily transformed to a sort of mystic purple. Fortunately there was no mirror, so she only saw the transformation of other complexions, not of her own. But the illumination did not draw her in to see *The Hound with Gleaming Eyes* and *Other People's Wives*, with Full Supporting Programme, and only served to accentuate the darkness before and beyond.

Milly Brown had a second reason for not entering the cinema. She had left the Blue Stag, after her simple meal there, to stroll and not to spend. Her practical mind was trying to grasp and elucidate the strange situation in which she had suddenly found herself, and to get a useful angle on her humble employer. Her eyes were serene, but her mind was troubled. She liked Simon Smith, and she wondered whether he would be able to carry out his queer mission, even with her encouragement. If he needed

53

more than encouragement, she hoped he would ask for it, but she did not want to intrude her personal curiosity or advice.

Curiosity led her neat feet, however, in the direction of the King's Head, and as she neared the hotel and regarded its flat, gloomy exterior, she wondered whether Simon were behind any of the windows she saw, and what he was doing. " I'm perfectly sure he would have scrapped Mrs. Grundy—who's dead anyhow, isn't she ?—and suggested my staying at the same hotel," she reflected, " if there hadn't been a very definite reason against it. And *what* was the reason ? "

She paused just before reaching the entrance. A man was coming out of the hotel in a hurry. The hurry was so great that as he turned towards her from the steps they nearly collisioned.

" Sorry ! " he muttered, and steered rapidly round her.

" Nasty person ! " she decided. " Did somebody else he barged into like that smash his nose ? "

She resumed her way, glancing through the entrance as she passed by. The only thing she glimpsed was a yawning maid. Then, though it was still early, she decided to return to her own hotel and get to bed. If the morrow were going to be as exciting as to-day, the best preparation was a long night's sleep.

But before she went to sleep, she sat up in bed and jotted in her note-book :

" Well, no accidents so far, but I'm not betting on to-morrow ! Reached Brackham 3.30. One-horse town. S. combed whole place, but did no business. Shops closed 6. Took him to King's Head, saw him fixed up there, and came to Blue Stag. Booked cheapest room. Also smallest. Couldn't swing a mouse in it. Fortunately never had any inclination to. Note : keep sense of humour going. Helpful to both of us. Query : Has S. got any ? Meal, fried egg and bread and butter. Latter thick enough to gag the best. Query : am I lonely ? Answer : don't know. Took a stroll at 8.45. If ever decide to commit suicide, shall return to Brackham to do it. Make departing life a pleasure. Went by King's Head. Query : did I hope to see S. ? Answer : Yes. But all I saw was a man with half a nose who bumped into me as he left the hotel, and yawning maid. Back to this room. Into this bed. Query : Is bed lumpy ? Answer : YES. Good-night."

Then she slipped the note-book under her pillow and, despite the lumps, slept.

But Simon, in his much larger bed at the other end of the town, lay long awake. He was less able than Milly to control an imaginative mind, and twice he relit his candle in the hope that a sight of the material objects around him would dispel his disturbing flights of fancy. One of the flights of fancy was Thomas Raikes with a pitchfork and a tail. Another was a limitless void in which a telephone was ringing. . . . He had again tried to telephone to Mr. Mildenhall just before coming up to bed. . . . But the first material object he always saw was the grotesque green elephant, which brought him no relief. Nor was he consoled by the reflection of his own candle-lit face in the mirror above the elephant. What he needed for his comfort was Milly Brown sleeping peacefully in the next room, instead of at the other end of the town.

At last he fell into a fitful doze. He was awakened
by a sound at his door. Was someone trying the
handle ? He thanked God that he had locked the
door, and lit the candle again.

"Who's there ? " he called.

His voice disappointed him. He had intended it
to be bold, but it had been weak and wobbly. Nevertheless, it proclaimed his wakefulness, and he could
have sworn he heard soft steps moving away along
the passage.

He slipped out of bed.

" Of course, I expect the whole thing's my imagination, really ! " he lied to himself, in order to secure
the courage to cross to the door. " I must have been
dreaming or something."

At the door he listened tensely. Hearing nothing,
he applied his ear to the keyhole, after softly remov-
ing the key. Still nothing. No, something ! What ?
A sort of drip. . . . Well, what was that to worry
him ? He recalled that a tap leaked in the bathroom
just across the corridor.

Like many people who are not built to deal with
trouble, he imagined that the correct thing to do in a
crisis was the thing that was least pleasant. Following this principle, he inserted the key again, turned it
quietly, and threw the door open. He fully expected
someone to jump on him, but no one did. The
passage, faintly illuminated by pale moonlight that
filtered through an unseen window, proved empty.
He closed the door again, locked it, and felt a little
sick.

About to return to bed, he found himself staring
at the door in the wall on the right of the green
elephant. The door of the hanging cupboard. He

had examined this when he had first entered the
room, and it had been as empty as the passage, but
somehow it held a horrible fascination for him, and
he felt he could not get back to bed until he had
examined it again. Taking a sip of water to ease his
dry throat, he went to the door to open it. It was
locked, and the key was gone.

" This is nasty," he thought.

He knew it had been unlocked before dinner, and
that the key had been there then. He knew that
he had not locked it afterwards, or removed the
key. What he could not recall was whether the key
had been in the door when he got into bed. He had
not noticed the key's presence or absence after his
original examination.

" Probably the maid locked the cupboard when
she was fixing my room," he decided. He had to
decide something. " She was in the room when I
went down to dinner. Or she may have come in one
of the times I was trying to telephone. Anyway—
of course—there's nothing really to worry about ! "

All the same, he fixed a chair in front of the cupboard door before he returned to bed and blew out
the candle. After which, weariness beat anxiety,
and he fell into a deep sleep which lasted till a knock
on the door woke him up.

A voice informed him that it was the maid with
his shaving water. He looked at his watch, discovering to his consternation that it was half-past eight.
And Milly was due to arrive with the car at nine !
He bounded out of bed, and, unlocking the door,
bashfully permitted the maid to see him in his
pyjamas. She, on her side, displayed no emotion.
She had seen hundreds of pyjamas.

" A nice day," she said, as she placed the hot water on the washstand. " Breakfast's being served in the coffee-room, whenever you want it."

" I'll be down almost at once," he answered. " I have to leave at nine."

" You'll have to hurry then," she commented, but made no effort to assist him by departing. " Overslep', didn't you ? I knocked once before."

" Yes, I expect I must have," he replied.

" That's having all those visitors last night," she went on, unintelligently. " Not that they stayed late."

" No. What ? I didn't have a lot of visitors ! "

" Aren't I awful, the way I exaggerate ? I meant two."

" Only one," he corrected her.

To his surprise, she shook her head.

" You *have* overslep' ! " she retorted. " Fancy forgetting ! Why, first there was that one who came while you was at dinner, and then there was the other one who left soon afterwards."

Simon stared at her in astonishment.

" What do you mean ? " he exclaimed. " The one who left soon afterwards—he didn't stay long—*was* the one who came while I was at dinner ! "

" Well, now *I* don't know what *you're* talking about," she returned. " Are you one of those jokers ? Some people are never satisfied unless they're pulling somebody else's leg ! The one who came while you were at dinner was a tall man, with a black moustache. I showed him up myself. ' Don't disturb him,' he said, ' I'll wait in his room, and you can let him know I'm here when he's finished,' he said. That's what I told you, didn't I ? But the other one—the one I saw going—he was smaller, and had a funny nose ! "

Simon continued to stare. Was the maid mad, or was he ?

" What time did you see him go ? " he asked.

" Well, it was a bit after eight," she answered. " I was just coming along the passage to go downstairs."

" And what time did the other man—the one with the moustache—come ? "

" Oh, dinner was just starting. A bit after seven."

Simon recalled the tall man he had seen entering the hotel as he had passed into the dining-room.

" But you didn't see *him* go ? "

" No." A bell rang. " Oh dear, there's No. 9 ! One of the impatient ones ! "

She darted away.

Completely bewildered, Simon closed the door, and sat down on his bed for five minutes. Then he suddenly wrenched his mind from the past to the present, and realised that he only had twenty minutes in which to shave, dress, and have breakfast. Performing all these operations at emotional speed, he found himself ready with four minutes still to spare, and he used the time in another effort to ring up Mr. Mildenhall. The morning attempt was as fruitless as had been those of the evening before.

As he left the telephone-box and walked to the entrance, the clock struck nine, and Milly appeared with the car.

CHAPTER SEVEN

THE PRICE OF FORGETFULNESS

THE SIGHT of Milly's cheerful face temporarily dispelled Simon's gloom. She gave him a sense of solidarity as well as of companionship, seeming to supply the qualities he lacked, and he felt that nothing could really go wrong while she was by his side. The one difficulty with an otherwise perfect team was that he was not free to confide in her. His oath of secrecy stood in the way, and since he had already betrayed Mr. Mildenhall's trust in one particular, he was painfully anxious not to add to his sins. He wanted, indeed, to prove to Mr. Mildenhall at the conclusion of the week that he had justified his one deceit, and had acted in the interest of Nugum Limited by using his initiative and bringing Milly along.

" Good-morning ! " she called, as he descended the hotel steps with his small luggage.

The boy was not by to assist him, for that experienced youth had marked " No. 6 " as no good for a tip, and he never volunteered for work without reward. Simon had left sixpence on the washstand, however, for the maid.

" Good-morning," he replied. " How did you sleep ? "

" Like a top ! And you ? "

" Eh ? Oh—not too bad. Well, as a matter of fact, I slept like a top, too, once I got off properly. I only woke up half an hour ago."

" Really ? Then I congratulate you on the smoothness of your chin," she laughed. " Only I hope you didn't forgo your breakfast so you could shave ? "

" Oh, no, I managed both," he smiled back. " And I also had another shot at telephoning to——"

He stopped short. Should he have said that ? She gave him a quick glance, but noting his expression as he took the seat beside her did not pursue the subject. Instead she asked :

" Well ? Where ? "

He brought his instruction sheet from his pocket to confirm his recollection that the second town was Chanton. As neither of them knew it, she drew the map from its pigeon-hole. He noticed, with too much admiration, that everything was polished and tidy in the front of the car, every tiniest accessory in place. As they studied the map together, he tried unsuccessfully not to be conscious that their heads were close. The pleasant proximity somewhat blurred his vision, and it was she who eventually picked out the name, some distance north-east of Brackham.

" About seventy miles," she reported, after a quick calculation. " Shall I get you there in one hour or two ? "

" Three," he suggested.

" That will shorten the working day ! "

" Yes, but it won't unsteady my nerves for the work. And besides, even though this is a business trip, Miss Brown, there's no reason why we shouldn't enjoy the scenery, is there ? "

She smiled, and let in the clutch.

Simon always looked back on the drive from Brackham to Chanton as the most peaceful period of that amazing week. Travelling at a comfortable thirty, they went through country that was gently undulating or picturesquely flat, and the disturbances of the previous night dissolved in the sunshine, as though banished from a better world. The ghosts were to return, and to increase, but he did not know this. Or perhaps he merely closed his eyes to an obvious possibility.

Sometimes they talked, though never about business. He was never good at conversation, but she had a fund of pleasant nonsense, as if to balance her practical side, and often drew responses that surprised him. At other times they sat silent, relaxed and content. If all life could have been like this, the world would have been a happy place to have been born into! Once, however, when he did not answer a remark, she turned her head and noticed a grave expression.

"Anything the matter?" she asked.

"Eh? No!" he replied, hastily. "Look at that blackbird on that scarecrow over there!"

What he had been thinking of was his omission to ask the maid at the King's Head about the locked cupboard. He had forgotten to do so through his surprise at her information about the two visitors; and he had just remembered that he had forgotten. . . .

"I think, Mr. Smith," said Milly, "that when I ask inconvenient questions, the best plan will be to say Subject Barred!"

He coloured slightly.

"I—I hope I wasn't rude," he murmured.

"You couldn't be," she answered. "All I'm doing is to tell you that I know when you're worried, and it's waste of energy trying to put me off ! Look at that rabbit on that chimney-pot ! "

They reached Chanton at half-past eleven, and found it an improvement on Brackham. It was a small market town, full of rustic energy, but whether the local population would show any enthusiasm for gum was yet to be proved. As it was early, they changed their previous procedure, and decided to fix on their hotels before starting business. Simon's, this time, was the Golden Crown, easily found as the inn sign stuck out prominently in the cobbled High Street.

" Shall I wait, as before ? " she asked, as they stopped. " Or shall I find my own hotel, and come back ? "

" Yes, that's the idea," he replied. " And then we'll get busy."

" Half an hour ? "

" I'll be ready."

" Of course, you'll want your luggage out before I go."

She turned her head and looked towards the back seat.

" I say—shouldn't there be three things ? " she exclaimed.

" Yes, two bags and a box," he answered.

" I only see one bag and a box."

Following her gaze, Simon stared in consternation.

" Do you remember putting both bags in ? " inquired Milly.

" I can't say I do," muttered Simon.

" Do you remember putting only one bag in ? "

Deeply humiliated, Simon did remember that !

He had meant to return to his bedroom for the
second bag, and in the confusion of the departure
had forgotten.

" Well, there's only one thing to do," said Milly.
" I must go back for it."

" What—seventy miles ? "

" You've got to have it, haven't you ? It's the
firm's property ! Don't look so glum ! I won't stop
and enjoy the scenery this time, and I'll be back here
round about three. Meanwhile, you'll have to carry
on with half your samples."

" I'm a mug, and you're a brick," he murmured,
penitently.

" Nonsense, I should have checked up on it," she
retorted. " Don't forget, we're a team, and share the
kicks with the glory ! " She added, " And the sooner
I go, the sooner I'll return. Mind you meet me with
good news ! "

A few seconds later she had turned the car and
vanished, and as Simon watched her depart, seeming
to take the sunlight with her, he decided that no
man had ever been more completely punished for
his folly.

He entered the Golden Crown with a little sigh.
The proprietor, a large, red-faced man, was in his
shirt-sleeves, smoking a pipe.

" A room ? Yes, plenty," he responded to
Simon's inquiry. " Large, small, front, back, with
running water or without."

" I think my room has been already booked,"
answered Simon.

" Oh, has it ? What name ? "

" Grainger."

" Ah, Grainger. Yes, that's right. Number Six."

A queer little chill went through Simon. Six again! Was this a mere coincidence? He hoped sincerely that it was. Already he was beginning to hate the number!

The proprietor conducted him to the room himself, and Simon had to admit that, judged superficially, the number was the only thing wrong with it. The furniture was homely and comfortable, and in addition to the bed there were two armchairs and a couch. The fireplace was not screened by any sinister animal, and contained nothing more offending than a fan of blue crinkled paper. The china was also blue, and the window provided a view of a picturesquely untidy garden, instead of a wall and a chimney-pot. Best of all, there was no built-in cupboard!

" All right for you? " queried mine host.

" Very nice," answered Simon.

" Yes, everybody likes this room since we had it done up," said the proprietor, and added, with a grimace, " though it wasn't so popular just before! "

" Why not? "

" A fellow cut his throat here."

" Dear me! "

" That's why we had it done up. We changed the furniture round, too. The wife's idea. You see, the bed used to be in that other corner, and, well, that's where it happened. But there are some folk who come here who still refuse to sleep in No. 6. Silly, isn't it? "

" Er—idiotic," murmured Simon.

The proprietor eyed him contemplatively, and then glanced at his luggage.

R.N.S.   E

" Just staying the one night, I understand ? " he asked.

" That's right," nodded Simon.

" Commercial ? "

" Er—yes."

" I don't suppose you're selling anything *I* want ? "

" Gum," replied. Simon. " Nugum. Best on the market."

" Quite so, quite so," smiled the proprietor. " And my hotel's the best in the kingdom."

And he winked and departed.

Simon sat on the couch for a few minutes to collect himself and to arrange his thoughts. Like most people who are easily flustered, he needed periods for recovery to tidy up his mind after it had been upset. The couch, soft and comfortable, half facing the leafy view from the window, was a perfect spot for the operation ; nevertheless, he found the operation difficult. This was not, he told himself, because the corner where the bed used to be was near the couch. It was because the whole angle of his adventure was changing, and he was trying to adjust himself to its new aspects.

For one thing, he discovered that his enthusiasm for his job—at least, for the business side of it—was being hampered by a growing sense that the business side was unimportant. The important part of his work should have been the attempt to secure orders for Nugum between the opening and closing of shops, and it was here that he had expected to centralise his energy and his interest. But the evening visitors, of whom he had only so far received one, already loomed above all else, together with the perplexities with which he could not dissociate them ; and instead of thinking, " How can I persuade people to buy Nugum ? " he thought, " Was Thomas Raikes really a business man, as he was supposed to be ? "—" Who was the other fellow, with the black moustache, who the maid said had gone to my room first ? "—" Who locked that cupboard and took the key ? "—" Did any one try to get into my room last night, or was it my imagination ? "—" Will somebody else try to get into this room to-night ? "—" What will this evening's visitor be like ? "—" Why was I chosen for this job, when I am obviously such a fool ? "—" Was *that* the reason ? " (an arresting thought, this, as startling as humiliating).—" Where is Mr. Mildenhall ? "

Compared with all these considerations, the mere obtaining of orders seemed as the molehill to the mountain !

Still, until these other considerations swept him off his unsteady feet, there was nothing to do but to carry on, and he suddenly jumped up from the couch, reprimanded himself for wasting time, locked the black box in a drawer, and sallied forth into Chanton's cobbled High Street with his solitary brown bag.

He passed an anxious, depressing day. The time dragged till three o'clock, even though at one shop a kindly woman told him to call again at four when her husband, whom she felt sure would be interested, would be in. He forgot to have any lunch, and was back at the Golden Crown a quarter of an hour before the time mentioned by Milly.

" I don't suppose my chauffeuse has come back here yet ? " he asked the proprietor casually.

The proprietor looked up from the racing news at the rather impressive question. You wouldn't have thought a mild little fellow like this would have a chauffeuse, now !

" No one's been here for you," he answered.

" Well, if she comes any time when I'm out, please ask her to wait," said Simon.

" Right," replied the proprietor. " Have you heard what won the 1.30 ? "

Simon had not the slightest idea. The only time he was interested in was three.

The market clock not far away struck thrice. No familiar car appeared in the High Street. He waited in the hotel entrance till a quarter-past, then dived to a shop he had marked five minutes away, had a breathless interview with a gentleman who eventually turned out to be a customer, and dived back again. Still no familiar car. He waited till four. When the market clock clanged the hour, he suddenly recalled that he had to see the husband of the kindly woman. He arrived there, hot, ten minutes late, convinced that his tardiness would destroy the slender hopes of business. But the kindly woman informed him that her husband had telephoned to her that he would not be in till five. So back he went once more to the hotel, and still Milly had not returned.

At five o'clock he paid his third visit to the shop of the kindly woman. To his amazement, her husband was there, and to his greater amazement he received an order for three dozen tubes of Nugum, A Quality. The order was like a little ray of sunshine glinting unexpectedly through a bank of clouds believed to be impregnable. But the ray went out when, back at the Golden Crown, he found that Milly had still not returned. Already she was two and a half hours late.

Had she had an accident ? The idea grew into an obsession as the minutes dragged by. He had only known her for about thirty hours, yet she already figured in his estimation as the most dependable person in existence, and it seemed that nothing short of catastrophe could prevent her from keeping an appointment. Suddenly he thought of phoning up the hotel at Brackham. He tried three times, but it was always engaged. That, in itself, seemed odd. The King's Head was not an hotel one would ordinarily associate with urgent telephonic activity. Between these fruitless calls, he tried again to get on to Mr. Mildenhall, with the usual no-reply result.

At seven he discovered that he felt weak. Ascribing this at first to worry, he afterwards added the cause of hunger, recalling that he had had nothing to eat since breakfast, and that the breakfast itself had been hurried. He went into the dining-room, chose a table as far away from other diners as he could—there were not many—and decided resolutely to forget everything but food. The decision broke down almost immediately, and the meal was dogged by two insistent visions.

The first was of Milly lying unconscious in a ditch. The car was upside-down in another ditch. She lay below the level of the road, and people passed by constantly without noticing her. For some unspecified reason, they did not notice the car either.

The second vision was of the empty room in Mr. Mildenhall's flat, with only the photograph of a beautiful girl to listen to the ringing of a telephone-bell.

As on the previous evening, he lingered over his meal, because when thoughts are rampant anything is better than doing nothing. And, also as on the previous evening, just as he was finishing, someone entered the dining-room with a message for him. It was the proprietor.

" She's come," he announced, as he reached Simon's table.

" She ? " jerked Simon, jumping up.

" *And* a very attractive chauffeuse it is, if I may say so," added the proprietor, with a wink. " You know how to pick 'em ! "

" Where is she ? "

" Up in your room. Was that right ? She said you expected her."

In his room ? With his head in a whirl, Simon hastened up. A dark-eyed woman in a fur coat was on the couch waiting for him.

CHAPTER EIGHT

THE SECOND CALLER

" GOOD-EVENING," said the visitor.

" Er—good-evening," answered Simon.

He found her regarding him with vague amusement.

" Am I too early ? " she asked. " You expected me, didn't you ? "

" Yes, that's right," he replied quickly. " I knew you'd be coming, of course."

" Then why the surprise ? "

" Eh ? Well, as a matter of fact—just for the moment, I thought you might be somebody else."

" I hope I wasn't a disappointment ? "

To this blatant question he found no adequate reply. He murmured something, but did not recall afterwards what it was. She had, of course, been a great disappointment.

She accepted his lukewarm attitude complacently, and opened her coat, revealing a dark-green evening-frock. This seemed hardly appropriate to a business interview, and the sense of unreality that had marked the interview with Thomas Raikes on the previous evening was stronger now than ever.

" You're very cosy here," she remarked. " You know how to choose a good room." He refrained from commenting that the room had been chosen for him. " May I take off my coat ? It's hot."

" Yes, certainly," he replied.

71

She stood up, and waited. He advanced with
unwilling obedience to the obligations of the moment,
and removed the coat from her shoulders. They
were, he discovered, excellent shoulders, and she
laughed as he laid the coat over a chair.

" You are not a lady's man, Mr. Grainger,"
she said.

" I'm afraid not," he admitted.

" Well, perhaps that's as well, as this is a strictly
business interview." She laughed again as she sat
down. " So let us get to business. Have you had a
satisfactory day ? "

The question sounded absurd. So did his answer.

" I have secured one small order," he said.

" Then you've done better than I have," she
replied, " because I haven't secured any orders at
all. And so that's that, and let us get on to the
next."

If she were anxious to get the interview over, so
was he, but caution urged him not to be rushed.
Whatever attitude she chose to adopt, he decided
that it would be unwise for him to step outside his
alleged role, and he risked a businesslike frown.

" But you have something more to report, haven't
you ? " he inquired.

" Have I ? " She considered the point, then
smiled at him. " Yes, of course. The woman's
point of view. I believe the demand for Nugum
would be less disastrously absent if it were put up
in a more attractive form. Those tubes, for instance.
There's one in the pocket of my coat. Will you take
it out ? Perhaps I should have produced it before
to prove my credentials." He obeyed, and removed
the tube from the company of a little silk

handkerchief and a lipstick. "And bring it over here. Don't stand a mile off ! I can't speak to a man at a distance."

He advanced to the couch. She patted the place beside her, and he sat down against his will.

"That's better," she went on. "Now, then. Isn't this tube ugly ? Don't you agree ? It ought to be a pretty colour, something that strikes the eye to entice both the seller and the purchaser thereof."

"Well, that is certainly a point," he admitted.

"I'm glad you think so. What this tube needs is sex appeal. Ask Elizabeth Arden. There ! Is that enough ? I'm sure Mr. Mildenhall will be delighted when you write to him ! "

"He will also want your name," said Simon.

A faint smile flickered across her lips.

"Oh, yes—of course." But she did not supply it immediately. Instead she asked, casually, "By the way, who was it called on you last night ? "

The question disturbed him. It sounded innocent enough, but he was not sure that he ought to answer it. He had a feeling, too, that the casualness was assumed.

"I'm supposed to treat these interviews as strictly confidential," he said.

"And I am sure, Mr. Grainger, you do *all* you are supposed to do ! " she replied. "But, surely, there can be no harm in telling me this ? "

"I dare say not, but—well, I have been engaged for a week on trial, so maybe I am over-particular."

"I see. And Mr. Mildenhall told you not to mention any names ? " He was silent. "Well, over-conscientiousness is a good fault. Still, perhaps I can guess. Was it a man about an inch taller than

you, but not so good-looking ? " As Simon flushed,
she added, " And with a nose that had seen better
days ? "

" Suppose he was ? " murmured Simon.

The situation momentarily beat him. He was no
match for a woman.

" In that case, I'd be interested to know how you
got on together ? " she asked. " Don't look so
worried ! Did you find him agreeable ? "

" I—I am sure Mr. Mildenhall wouldn't want me
to discuss other members of the firm," he answered.

" Really, Mr. Grainger, you are most exceptionally
discreet ! " she exclaimed, but impatience was mixed
with the admiration. " Don't risk telling me, will
you, whether he knocked before he entered your
room, or whether you offered him a cigarette? Which,
by the way, you haven't offered *me* ! "

" Oh, I beg your pardon ! Yes, of course."

He fished a packet from his pocket, and she
extracted a cigarette. He tried not to notice her
prettiness. It did not interest him, but she possessed
little tricks by which she made one conscious of it.

" A match helps," she suggested.

He produced one, and after accepting the light
she blew the match out.

" Well, your discretion has one advantage," she
commented, as she leaned back in the couch and
puffed a perfect smoke-ring. " If you won't discuss
your last interview, you won't discuss this one !
Whatever happens between us will be strictly
entre nous ! Just the same, Mr. Grainger—do sit
down again, please—just the same, my inquiry
regarding your last visitor wasn't an idle one. May
I be quite frank ? "

"Yes, of course," he answered apprehensively. He had obeyed her request, and was again by her side.

"You realise, don't you?—I'm sure you do, because I can see you are a man of sense—you realise that this isn't—well—an *ordinary* business?"

"Isn't it?" he murmured.

"Surely you gathered that from Mr. Mildenhall?" she pressed.

"My instructions were only business instructions," he replied. "Those are all I have to carry out."

"I see. Then you are not conscious of anything unusual in your instructions? Is that so?"

"Yes. No. I mean, that is so," he said untruthfully.

"If you were asked to swear that on the Bible, you would do so?"

"I can't see how the necessity would arise."

"Shall I tell you something I *can* see? That you are a shocking bad liar! Which also suggests that you must be a shocking bad business man, since clever lying is the foundation of successful business life. I wonder why Mr. Mildenhall selected you?" She turned her head towards him, and studied him enigmatically. "You know, my opinion, Mr. Grainger, is that we should—trust each other more. Members of a firm have a duty to each other, as well as to their employer."

She moved a little closer to him. He found the scent she was using a little overpowering. Their arms touched, and he wondered how he could remove his without appearing too definitely rude.

"I'm not sure that I really know what you're

talking about," he said. " If I do my duty by my employer, I must be doing my duty by the others he employs."

" Not necessarily," she returned. " Suppose, for instance—I say just suppose, you know—suppose I thought it was my duty to warn you that, if you continue in Mr. Mildenhall's employment, you may run yourself into danger ? "

" Danger ? What danger ? "

" I said, I was supposing it. Would you think I was wrong to Mr. Mildenhall—in showing this interest in you ? " Suddenly she added, " You are in danger, Mr. Grainger ! You'd better cut out of this at once. I can carry on for you."

He stared at her in astonishment and indignation. He did not think much of himself, but for all her small compliments, she evidently thought less !

" That would transfer the danger to you," he pointed out. " Do you expect I'd do that ? "

" But I would be in no danger."

" Before I could judge that I'd have to know what the danger was, wouldn't I ? "

" I'm not asking you to judge—I'm telling you ! " As he made no reply she changed the subject impatiently. " Last night's visitor—did he give you any message for me ? "

" Message ? No ! "

" You just did your business together, and then he went ? "

" Yes. And—er—perhaps we ought to finish our own business together——"

" So that *I* can go ? "

" I didn't say that ! "

" But you meant it ! Or didn't you ? Perhaps,

after all, Mr. Grainger, I am not reading you right ?
After we have finished our business, the evening will
still be young. Shall we spend it together ? From
what I've seen of this town it doesn't seem to offer
much in the way of excitement, but perhaps with
a bottle of bubbly we could provide our own ? "
Now she smiled at him deliberately, and touched his
knee with a slender, ringed finger. " I have plenty
of time. Have you ? "

He did not answer at once, and she misinterpreted
his hesitation.

" Yes, let's have some fun ! " she exclaimed. " I
am quite convinced that you do not get enough,
and as for me, well, I'm thoroughly in the mood !
If you are not a lady's man, it's time you took
lessons ! I'm quite a good teacher—that is, when
I'm really interested. I'll tell you how to begin.
Don't suddenly seize me and plaster me with
kisses. *I* shouldn't mind, but the emotion would
probably overcome you, and you'd be no good for
the rest of the evening. Start slowly, and work up !
You might commence, for instance, by paying me a
little compliment ? " She gave him the chance by
adding, " If, of course, you think I'm worthy of
one ? "

Ninety-nine men out of a hundred would have
considered her worthy of one and would have
welcomed the chance to say so, but Simon's hesitation had not been due to temptation. It had been due
to his inability to think of the right words to
indicate that he was the hundredth. Now the words
came to him. Her blatant method excused his own.

" I'm afraid you'll think me very rude," he said,
" but I have work to do to-night, so if you'll just

tell me your name, which you haven't done yet——"

" I think you exceedingly rude," she interrupted. The smile had vanished from her face, and her expression was black.

" I—I am sorry."

" You are not in the least sorry. Very well, let us get this over. You have something for me ? "

" Mr. Mildenhall's instructions. Yes."

" My name is—Edith Searle. S-e-a-r-l-e, Searle."

She held out her hand. It was no longer caressing. It was acquisitive. Her whole attitude had changed as violently as her expression. He produced the envelope from the box. She took it quickly and ungraciously, and rose from the couch.

" Don't trouble about my cloak," she said. " I can put it on myself."

That was her last word. In ten seconds she was out of the room. But Simon heard her pause outside and tear open the envelope before her footsteps faded away along the passage.

CHAPTER NINE

" DEAR MR. MILDENHALL———"

ON the previous evening, after the departure of
Thomas Raikes, Simon had gone to the bed on which
that unpleasant individual had sat and had smoothed
away his impression. The impression made by
Edith Searle on the couch was even less desirable,
but it was also less visible, and after he had stared
at it for a minute with a sort of hateful fascination,
it effaced itself through some inner impulse of the
couch's springs, till all that remained of Edith
Searle were her memory and her scent.

The memory would stay, but Simon attempted to
hasten the departure of the scent by opening the
window wide. Then he left the room, and went to
the hotel telephone. As he asked for Mr. Mildenhall's number he felt he was merely obeying a fruitless routine, and it gave him no surprise that his
effort to connect with his employer ended in the
usual failure. " I suppose the phone isn't out of
order ? " he asked the operator. " No, I've been
ringing them," came the answer, " but they don't
reply."

Returning to his room, he wrote a letter. It was
the most difficult letter he had ever written, and it
took him till nearly midnight. He tore up, and then
burned, four unsatisfactory efforts, and even the
fifth did not satisfy him, but his mind was too
muzzy for further attempts and after reading it

through, he decided to send it. It began with a description of his endeavours to obtain orders, with his one success at Chanton, and with his hope that the experience he was gaining would produce more results on the morrow and be of ultimate service to the firm. " I appreciate this chance you are giving me," he wrote, " and I am determined to justify it if I can." And then he expressed the earnest hope that Mr. Mildenhall would regard the remarks that followed as an expression of this desire, and would treat the said remarks as strictly confidential.

" They concern the two representatives I have so far interviewed in accordance with your instructions," he went on, " and whose names I endeavoured to telephone to you. As already mentioned, my efforts in this direction were not successful, though I tried to get on to you repeatedly. The representatives were, respectively, Mr. Thomas Raikes and Miss (or Mrs.) Edith Searle. It seems my duty to inform you that I was not impressed with either of these persons, though whether my personal opinion is of any value you will have to decide for yourself.

" First, as to Mr. Raikes. I informed him, in response to his inquiry, that I had not as yet procured any orders, and that, as already mentioned, I had only been afforded two hours in Brackham for this purpose. When I questioned him concerning his own activities on behalf of the firm, he told me to inform you that Leicester was a wash-out but Nottingham was O.K. I quote his own words. He added the suggestion that you might be well advised to start a branch in Nottingham. But in passing this information on to you, Sir, I feel it necessary to pass on also my impression that Mr. Raikes did not conduct himself in the strictly businesslike manner I should have expected, nor did he appear to take our business as seriously as, I imagine, is necessary for successful dealing. Indeed, at moments he was almost levitous. In expressing this personal view to you, please realise, Sir, that I myself shall take no exception to anything Mr. Raikes may himself write to you concerning me. Quite frankly, I doubt whether he was any more impressed with me than I was with him, and he is equally entitled to convey his opinion to you.

"Second, as to Miss (or Mrs.) Edith Searle. I reported my day's activities to her, referring to the one order I have secured, as already mentioned, and in return she informed me that she had done no business at all. Quite frankly, this did not surprise me, for she seemed to take the business side of our interview with as little seriousness as Mr. Raikes had shown. She did make one suggestion, and in fairness I am bound to say there may be something in it. She proposes that we put up our Gum in some more attractive form, and quoted the case of Elizabeth Arden products. It occurred to me that purchasers of gum would not have quite the same angle as purchasers of, say, powders and lipstick, but her idea may be worth your consideration, and I regretted that she advanced the idea with a certain underlying humour which, to me, indicated a lack of confidence in it.

"Of course, Sir, when you engaged these two representatives you were doubtless aware of qualifications which may not have emerged in the interviews described, but since I am now a member of

the Firm, with an obligation to act only in the
Firm's interest, I would like to suggest, if I may,
that should you have waived the matter of testi-
monials in their cases, as you did in my own, you
now take some step, if you have not already done so,
which I admit you may have, to ensure that they are
fully qualified for the jobs they have undertaken.
Should this be a presumption on my part, please
forgive me.

" Adverting to my unsuccessful attempts to get
into telephonic touch with you, if this continues
perhaps you would telephone to me yourself at one
of my next hotels, should you have any comments
to offer or further instructions to give. But if I do
not hear from you, I will continue as I am going,
while hoping for more successful results. Believe me,
yours faithfully, S. SMITH."

He posted the letter as a clock chimed midnight,
and returned to his hotel with no repose in his
breast.

CHAPTER TEN

WHAT HAPPENED TO MILLY

SIMON's last operation before getting into bed was to repeat the precaution of locking the door, but so far as he knew no one tried to enter his room in the night. His dreams, however, were almost as disturbing as wakeful horrors, and considerably more embarrassing. The too attractive Edith Searle wandered through his filmy fancies like a super-vamp, and his own behaviour displeased him intensely when he awoke and recalled it. "Why am I dreaming about her?" he demanded of his pillow, deeply humiliated. "I don't like the woman!" And then promptly went to sleep again to dream of her even more violently.

He awoke with a headache. The red-faced proprietor commented on his pale appearance over breakfast. "Bless me if you don't look like the morning after the night before," he remarked. "Did you sleep all right?"

"Yes, thank you," lied Simon.

"Well, you look like the morning after the night before," answered the proprietor.

"So you've just said," Simon reminded him.

"Well, that's what you look like. You didn't have bad dreams, did you? About that chap I told you of who committed suicide?"

Simon assured him, rather irritably, that he had not. The proprietor shook his head gloomily.

" What *I* take, when I'm feeling dicky, is a couple of aspirins," he said. " Yes, but I know something better than that to-day. Here's your tonic. Rusty Sam for the 3.30."

Then, to Simon's relief, he was called away.

But he was back a few minutes later, with a newspaper in his hand.

" Here we are," he exclaimed. " Rusty Sam, eight to one. Back that to win, and Woman Hater for a place. Yes, and I'm a woman hater this morning," he added. " Just been called a liar by one ! "

" Have you ? " murmured Simon, uninterested.

" Saucy little chit ! " said the proprietor. " Up she drives and asks for Mr. Smith. ' No one here of that name,' I tell her. ' Yes, he arrived here yesterday,' she says pertly, just as if I didn't know my own business ! ' The only person who arrived here yesterday,' I retort, ' was a Mr. Grainger——' "

Simon did not wait to hear any more. He bounced up from the table, nearly knocking the astonished innkeeper over, and raced to the lobby. There he nearly knocked Milly Brown over.

" I'm so glad you're back—where have you been ? —are you all right—— ? " he blurted out.

She looked at him searchingly. Her face was flushed, and although she also was glad to be back, Simon divined that her colour was not entirely due to her pleasure at the meeting. There was a new look in her eye as she answered,

" Yes ! Are *you* all right ? "

" Quite," he replied. " I say—is anything the matter ? "

" We'll talk in the car," she said. " Have you had your breakfast ? Can you leave quickly ? At once ? "

He stared at her.

" Of course. Only why ? "

" Tell you later. Hurry. I'll be waiting outside."

The next moment she was gone. Simon turned, to see the proprietor emerging from the coffee-room.

" Can I have my bill, please ? " he jerked.

" Aren't you going to finish your meal ? " inquired the proprietor.

" Eh ? I have finished it. I wasn't very hungry. What ? Oh, I thought you said something. I'll be down in a moment."

The proprietor looked after him as he raced up the stairs. Then he turned and looked towards the street. He often recalled this unusually hurried departure, which he now attributed, not to business, but to some complication vaguely summed up in the words, " Cherchez la femme ! " A scented beauty in the evening, and a chic little filly in the morning—the one knowing him by one name, and t'other by another——! The fellow didn't *look* like one o' them Gay Lotharios, but there you were ! You couldn't always judge men any more than horses by their looks !

The Gay Lothario came racing down the stairs again, looking anything but gay. He had a bag in one hand and a black box in the other, and he was going so fast that it was only the proprietor's dexterity that averted yet another collision.

" Hey ! Wait a moment ! " bawled the proprietor.

" Sorry ! Can't ! " gasped Simon.

" Sorry, but you'll have to ! " retorted the proprietor. " What about that bill ? "

Bills must be paid, whatever the urgency, and

Simon paused. The proprietor overcharged him a couple of shillings, considering this his due for early-morning flurry, and trusting that the flurry would conceal the inaccuracy. Which it did. Simon paid the amount demanded without question, and then shot out of the hotel without waiting for the change. The innkeeper blinked at his luck, and then returned to the coffee-room to finish the departed guest's breakfast.

If Simon had wasted no time inside, Milly wasted none outside. As soon as he had deposited his luggage in the back of the car—he was too flurried to notice that the case for which Milly had returned to Brackham was not there—and had taken his seat beside her, the car began to move, and in two minutes they were in the open road and the little market town was slipping away behind them. Then he asked:

" Well ? What is it ? What happened to you ? "

" Not just yet," she put him off again. " Let's get somewhere ! Am I on the right road for your next town ? "

Curbing his anxious curiosity, he answered:

" I don't know. It's Bulchester."

" Where's the map ? "

She stopped the car and took the map out of its pigeon-hole. In spite of her excitement, her finger was steady as she moved it across a county till, with almost uncanny accuracy, it stopped at the place it was seeking.

" Here we are ! " she exclaimed. " Bulchester. About forty miles. And we're right for it. We can be there by ten—if we want to."

" Don't we want to ? " he inquired.

" Yes, I expect so," she replied after a little pause, during which she replaced the map and started the car again. " But you'll have to hear what I've got to tell you before you decide."

" Well, I'm waiting to hear."

" Yes, I know. Only we need a nice quiet spot. We'll go a few more miles and then get off the main road."

As she entered top gear, the raucous noise of a speeding motor-cycle sounded behind them, and her lips tightened. The needle of the speedometer rose rapidly to forty-five and fifty, but the motor-cyclist was not going to be beaten by a small saloon. He came whizzing up behind them, passed them, and triumphantly gave them his dust. Milly's lips relaxed, and a faint, self-admonishing smile replaced their tightness.

Bursting to ask questions, Simon restrained himself, and no word was spoken till they had turned off the main road into a descending lane. Half a mile down the lane was a bend, and just beyond the bend was a gate into a field.

" This'll do," said Milly.

When the car had stopped, she got out. He followed her through the gate, and they sat down under a hedge, with a view of gently-rolling country ahead of them. Simon often thought of that field, and of the cows in the field beyond, chewing their cuds without, apparently, a trouble in the world. There was something, after all, in being a cow. . . .

" Cigarette ? " asked Milly.

He gave her one, and lit one for himself. Then she said:

" Now for it, Mr. Smith. And I'm afraid it's going to be nasty. But of course it'll all work out all right in the end, so don't forget that, will you ? "

" No, I won't forget it," he answered. " And here's something *you* needn't forget. Whatever it is, I'll see you through it."

" See—*me* through it ! "

" Well, I expect you knew that, anyway."

She gave him a queer look.

" But I'm not in any trouble, Mr. Smith."

" I'm glad."

" And if what I'm going to tell you brings *you* any trouble, I'll see *you* through it. Shall I blurt it out ? Might as well. A man was found dead in your room at the Brackham hotel after you left."

Simon's mouth opened, but no words came.

" I guessed there was some sort of trouble on as soon as I got near the hotel," she went on. " There was a policeman outside, and a small knot of people. That was why I didn't stop. I continued past the hotel, and turned a corner. Then I stopped, and heard two women talking by a pillar-box."

" Yes, but wait a minute ! " interposed Simon, finding his voice at last. " This is terrible, but it has nothing to do with me——"

" Well, you don't need to tell me that ! "

" I don't need to tell anybody that ! The person —whoever it was—must have gone into the room after I'd left."

He stopped short, as she shook her head.

" How do you know he didn't ? " he demanded.

" He was there all night," she answered grimly. " Locked in a cupboard."

Again Simon's mouth opened, and again no words

came. His vest grew suddenly damp. In the cupboard . . . in the *cupboard*. . . .

" Better let me finish my say," said Milly quietly and sympathetically, " and then you can have yours. I got my first news from those two gossiping women, and they were so engrossed in their conversation that they didn't notice me at all. I pretended to be doing something or other—I took out our map, as a matter of fact—but my ears were well open, and—well, I'll repeat what they said, as well as I can remember.

" Something like this. ' Yes, I've just come from the hotel, and it gave me quite a turn when I heard it,' one of them said. ' You see, one time I slept in that room—Number Six—and so I could just picture it. Why, the very dress I've now got on, I hung it in that cupboard ! ' Then the other said, ' But you don't really mean he was in the cupboard ? ' And the first one said, ' Yes, and it was locked, and the key had gone.' ' Then how did they get in it ? ' the other one asked, and the first one answered, ' The maid wanted to open it ; she said it hadn't been locked on the night before, so they forced it, and when the doctor came, he said the man had been dead several hours, over twelve——' "

" Twelve hours ! " gasped Simon. " Then—he *must* have been there all night ! "

" He was," nodded Milly solemnly. " I won't go on with their conversation. I'll tell just you what else I found out—from them and other sources, though I was careful not to seem personally interested."

" Why ? "

" Well—would it have been wise ? "

" I don't know."

" Nor did I ! I was as confused then as you must be feeling now. My one idea was to hear all I could, and then to get back to you before I did anything. I didn't even call at the hotel—I haven't brought back your bag."

" What else did you hear, please ? "

" I heard that the police want to get into touch with you, Mr. Smith."

" Yes—of course they would," murmured Simon, his brain spinning. " And—you could have helped them there."

" I know."

" But you didn't."

" No. I've asked myself why. I've told you I was confused, but I think perhaps this was one reason. Please don't misunderstand what I'm going to say— obviously you've had nothing to do with the beastly business—but there *is* some mystery connected with your job, isn't there ? So it seemed best that you should decide what to do. I didn't feel I knew enough to decide myself."

" Yes. I see. But—Miss Brown—I—I'm not *suspected* ! Am I ? "

Her answer was evasive.

" I've not spoken to a policeman, so I don't know."

" But what do you think ? "

" What do you ? " Suddenly she exclaimed, " Of course you're suspected ! We mustn't be ostriches and stick our heads in the sand." He liked that " we." " But this doesn't mean they think you've done it—it means that, till they find out more about you, they think you may have. They want to find you. They're looking for you. And, if you'll take my advice, you'll save a lot of trouble—both for the police and for yourself—by finding *them* ! "

" You mean, call at a police station, and report what I know ? "

" Yes." She gave him a sideways glance. " If you know anything. But call, even if you don't."

He stared at the grass. It did not help. It formed a green background for horrible pictures, when it should merely have been a pleasant environment for a man and a girl sitting together under a hedge. One of the pictures was of a locked door, and of himself standing before it, trying to open it. Another was of a dark shape behind the door, limp and silent. . . .

" They've got your bag, I expect," said Milly.

Another was of an unpleasant, cynical man, with a boxer's nose. . . .

" I heard someone say, ' He left his bag behind him in his hurry to be off.' "

" The man in the—the dead man ! " he exclaimed, with a catch in his voice. " What was he like ? Did you hear any description of him ? "

" Only that he had a black moustache," replied Milly.

Perspiration renewed itself on Simon's forehead. Black moustache ! The first man who had been shown into his room had had a black moustache ! The maid had said so ! And no one had seen that man go !

" Does that—convey anything to you ? " asked Milly.

" Yes," he whispered. " I—yes—it does."

She waited for something further, but it did not come. Partly to ease his mind of its immediate

agony, she reminded him that she had not yet
completed her story.

" Is there anything more ? " he gulped.

" Yes. I haven't told you why I was away so
long," she replied.

" Good Lord ! Fancy my forgetting that ! " he
said. " I—I was terribly worried. What kept you ? "

" Well, I stayed around for a bit, to get all the
details I could," she answered.

" Yes, of course."

" And then, in the afternoon, I started back.
And the car konked out, miles from everywhere.
That was just sheer bad luck. I can drive a car, but
I'm a duffer at mending one, and I couldn't find out
what the trouble was. I got towed to the next
village at last, found the world's worst garage, run
by the world's most disobliging man, and the car
wasn't ready till eight this morning. Of course, I
tried to phone you, but I was told that no one named
Smith was at the hotel, and when I insisted that
there was, they put up the receiver. That innkeeper's a bit of a fool, isn't he ? " she added. " He
even told me this morning that you weren't in the
place."

Simon smiled rather sheepishly as he was forced
to a confession.

" I—I have a business name," he said. " I have
to use it."

" Oh, so *that* explains it ! " exclaimed Milly.
" Another Mildenhall mystery ! "

" Er—well, yes."

She frowned, while staring at the tip of her shoe.

" Mr. Smith," she said, " I don't want you to tell
me anything you think you shouldn't—but it *would*

have helped, wouldn't it, if I'd known your second name ? Would St. Peter send you back from the gates of Heaven if you told it to me now ? "

He considered the matter, and decided that he would have a good argument to present to St. Peter, should objections be raised at the heavenly portals.

" My business name," he answered, " is Grainger."

" I will make a discreet note of it," she replied. " Of course—that's the name the innkeeper mentioned. " And now tell me something else. What did you think yesterday, when I didn't turn up ? "

" I thought perhaps you'd had an accident."

" Well, I did have."

" But I thought it might be to you, and not the car. I—I was terribly worried."

" Were you ? Well, of course, you would be. Your business needs a chauffeuse ! "

" I wasn't thinking of my business."

" No ? "

" I tried to telephone to the hotel, but I couldn't get on."

" Whew ! If you *had* got on, Mr. Smith ! " she exclaimed. " There'd have been some excitement ! Probably you couldn't because the hotel phone was more than usually busy yesterday."

" Yes, that was probably the reason," he agreed. " Well—if that's all—shall we be moving ? "

She turned her head, and they regarded each other gravely.

" Yes, better get it over," she said. " I dare say it won't be half as bad as it seems."

He tried, unsuccessfully, to share her optimism.

CHAPTER ELEVEN

SIMON LEARNS TO LIE

As FAR as he could recall, Simon had never spoken to a policeman in his life, and no policeman had ever spoken to him ; and to begin the acquaintance with a denial that he had murdered a man in a cupboard was no small ordeal. Milly's realisation of this caused her to complete the journey to Bulchester at a leisurely pace. They arrived, not at ten, but at eleven.

It was a silent journey. Milly's diary, which had succinctly recorded the previous day's experiences in the two words, " My God ! " related of the drive to Bulchester : " We sat and thought." But this was not strictly true in Simon's case. He spent most of the time trying to think, and finding it exceedingly difficult. And as they drew nearer and nearer their destination, the difficulty increased. The space inside his mind was mainly occupied by a vision of a police inspector whose attitude was not helpful. A second vision was of Henry Mildenhall, and this vision, from a different angle, was almost equally worrying. For some reason he could not explain, his personal interest in that strange personality increased till it almost became an obsession, and he found himself dwelling on his employer's point of view, even though he could not have defined it, as much as on his own. It was not merely that Mildenhall was trusting him. Perhaps it was the sense of trouble which had pervaded Mildenhall's

room like a heavy, unidentified scent. Mildenhall
was helping him ; he wanted to help Mildenhall.
He knew what trouble was himself, and he sym-
pathised with others who possessed that knowledge.

But the vision of Mildenhall differed from that of
the police inspector in another way as well. The
police inspector was in a dingy police station the
details of which were painfully clear, even though
Simon had never been inside a police station. The
details of Mildenhall's environment were vague and
nebulous. He was not in his room. All that resided
there were an unanswered telephone bell and a
large photograph of a lovely girl in evening-dress.
. . . Yes, that photograph was clear enough. It
was unreasonably, painfully clear. The silver frame
on the desk glinted round the charming features,
while the unanswered bell went on ringing. . . .
But Henry Mildenhall's features peered through a
dark cloud, and the dark cloud floated through
Simon's brain elusively, distractingly.

Before they entered Bulchester, however, Simon
had thought clearly about one point. If he had a
duty to Mildenhall, he also had a duty to Milly, and
he was exceedingly glad that she had not called at
the King's Head. Neither, he decided, was she going
to call at the police station. And when she suggested
that they inquired the way to it, he put his foot
down on the suggestion with unusual firmness.

" No, we're not going there first," he answered,
" and *you're* not going there at all."

" Why not ? " she asked, though she guessed the
reply.

" Because you've got to be kept right out of
this," he said.

She thought for a moment, then responded:

" That's nice of you, but how do you know I want to be kept out of it ? "

" It's not a question of what you want this time," he retorted. " It's what I want."

" Oh ! Really ? "

" Yes. Really."

She smiled, but shook her head. " I'm not sure that I can be kept out of it," she said.

" You can be kept out of it until you've got to be dragged into it," he responded, " which I hope won't be at all."

" I'm bound to crop up when you're questioned."

" I don't see that."

" Well, I do. They'll ask about your move-ments——"

" Yes, *my* movements——"

" And they'll want to know who moved you. ' How are you travelling ? Train or car ? ' ' Car.' ' Driving yourself ? ' What will you say to that ? "

Simon frowned. He had no idea what he would say to that. But he stuck to his point.

" There's quite enough trouble without anticipat-ing it, Miss Brown," he said, " and I don't believe they'll want to know that sort of thing. Why should they ? Anyhow, you are not going to the police station, or anywhere near it. My hotel is the Railway Hotel. Please drive me there. Or, no. Look ! " He pointed a little way ahead. " Isn't that another hotel, on the right ? Stop outside there, please, and if it seems any good you can book a room for the night. And—and I'll rejoin you when I come back."

She obeyed, reluctantly. The hotel sign, a dolphin,

cocked a malevolent eye at them as they drew up.
But the hotel itself looked respectable enough.

As he got out, she asked:

" Suppose you don't come back ? "

" Of course I'll come back ! " he replied.

" If you don't, I'll come after you," she answered,
" and that's a promise. What about your luggage ? "

" Please keep it till I return." Then he changed
his mind. " No, I'll take the bag with me." He was
not quite sure why, but had an idea it would look
better. " Just keep the box."

Was that wise ? The box contained the sealed
envelopes. Yet he did not want to take those to the
police station.

" I'll look after it," she said, noticing his hesitation.

" Yes. Thank you. Do."

Then, seizing the bag, and feeling suddenly a
little dizzy, he turned and hurried away.

Milly looked after him anxiously. " He won't be
selling much Nugum to-day ! " she reflected. Then
she went into the hotel, booked the cheapest room
they had, went up to it, and locked the box in the
only drawer that possessed a key. She put the key
into her bag.

The police station was at the other end of the
town. He was directed to it by a whistling errand
boy, whose care-free attitude he envied. As he
neared the station he discovered himself fighting
panic, and he fought it so hard that he did not
notice the station when he reached it, and walked
right past. Then he turned, recalling how he had
once walked past a dentist's door in much the same
fashion.

He nearly walked by the police station a second time, and stopped himself with an effort. " This won't do ! " he muttered, and turned towards the door with a ridiculous blitheness. A stout police-man almost filled the doorway.

" Er—can I come in ? " asked Simon.

The stout policeman eyed him with interest. He'd met plenty of curious people in his time, but never one who had requested permission to enter a police station as though it were a sort of favour.

" No one's stopping you," the policeman replied, not quite accurately. " Did you want to see some-one ? "

" Yes, please—the inspector," replied Simon, with even less accuracy. He did not want to see him at all.

The stout policeman stood aside, and jerked his thumb towards a half-open door. With a sense that he was walking into prison, Simon passed into a bare room. It was uncarpeted, and the only furni-ture was a bench under a window, a table strewn with papers and filing cabinets, a desk, and a chair. A red-cheeked sergeant was sitting in the chair.

" Yes ? " barked the sergeant.

" Er—are you the inspector ? " asked Simon.

" No, but I expect I'll do," replied the sergeant.

The sergeant did not appear to think highly of the visitor, and Simon decided that the inspector, whose existence he assumed, would be preferable. " What I've got to say is rather important, so I really think I ought to see the inspector."

This not very tactful observation did not increase the sergeant's affection for the visitor. He frowned as he responded :

" Well, come to that, I'm told important things

sometimes! Anyhow, the inspector isn't here. So—what is it?"

Simon cleared his throat, swallowed, and answered:

"It's—it's about the man who was found at the King's Head Hotel, Brackham. In the cupboard, you know."

The sergeant's attitude changed immediately. He glanced swiftly at a sheet on the desk, then back at Simon, whose face he studied with a new intentness. For a moment the sergeant concentrated on Simon's nose. Then he said, "Well? Yes?"

He fingered a pencil over a pad. Simon swallowed again. If his words were to be written down, he would have to choose them very carefully.

"I occupied that room—Room No. 6—on the night before," he said.

"Oh! You did!" exclaimed the sergeant. "Then your name—— ?"

"Smith. Simon Smith."

The sergeant again glanced at the sheet.

"That's not the name we've got," he commented.

"Eh? Oh, no, of course. The name you've got is Grainger, isn't it?"

"That's correct."

"Grainger is my business name."

"I see. And what's your business?"

"I am travelling for Nugum Limited." He held up his bag in confirmation. "A new kind of gum."

"And you left part of your luggage behind you, I understand?" queried the sergeant.

"Yes," nodded Simon. "I'm afraid I am rather absent-minded."

"Well, can I have your statement?"

" Yes, certainly. That's what I've come for."

" Right. Well ? "

" Of course, I don't know anything about the—
er—dead man," said Simon, " but I can give you
one or two facts that may help you. You see, someone called on me—and then I saw the dead man once
—before he was dead, that is, and provided it was
the same man—I thought at first he was the one
who was going to call——"

" One   moment,"   interrupted   the   sergeant.
" You've never made a statement to the police
before, have you ? "

" No, never."

The unnecessary information was emphatic.

" Then if I may suggest it, sir, just give me a
plain account of your actions from, say, the time
you arrived in Brackham. You arrived by car ? "

" Eh ? No ! "

The next moment Simon's heart almost stopped
beating. The next moment it raced. Had he said
" No " ? Yes, he had ! Lied to the police ? Yes, he
had ! Why ? His face remained defensively expres-
sionless while he discovered the reason. The reason
was that he had sworn to keep Milly out of the
business, and if he mentioned the car she would
undoubtedly be in it. He had lied instinctively, in a
subconscious panic, with neither thought nor intelligence ; and, having lied, he would have to stick to
his lie. . . . Car. . . . Car. . . . He had not arrived
by car. Then how had he arrived ? As the question
rose in his mind, the sergeant put it.

" By train," replied Simon.

" I see. By train," said the sergeant, and wrote
it down. " And what time would that be ? "

Time ! . . . What time ? . . .

" I can't say exactly," answered Simon. " Somewhere between three and four. In the afternoon," he added, with a sort of informative magnanimity.

" Yes ? Well ? And then ? "

" Then I called at a few shops with my samples."

" ' —with—my—samples,' " wrote the sergeant. " Yes ? "

" And then I went to the hotel."

" What time would that be ? "

" Oh—sixish. You see, the shops close at six."

" Quite so."

" I asked for a room. That is, for the room that had already been booked. Not that I suppose that matters. Let me know if I'm telling you more than is necessary——"

" You can't tell me more than is necessary," the sergeant assured him.

" Eh ? Thank you. Where was I ? Oh, yes. I went up to my room, and washed and all that, and presently I went down to dinner. I had a table at the far end of the room—oh, but wait a moment, I've forgotten something. Yes, this is important. While I was going into the dining-room, or coffee-room, I forget which it was called, but I suppose that doesn't matter—well, of course not—it was then that I saw a man who I think must be the man you found—I mean, who was found in the—the cupboard. He was just entering the hotel—that is, he had just entered—and I wondered if he was the person who was going to call on me. Then, after *that*, I took my table——"

" Just a moment again, sir. You were expecting a visitor, you say ? "

" Yes, a business one."

" Did you know him ? "

" No. If I had, I'd have known that this wasn't
the one—or was the one. I mean, whether he was or
not. Wouldn't I ? "

The sergeant rubbed his forehead, and then
admitted that he might.

" And he wasn't ? " he added, for confirmation of
a point that still seemed in doubt.

" Apparently not," replied Simon.

" Did you see him again ? "

" No. Only that once."

" Can you describe him."

" Only a little, I'm afraid. You see, I didn't see
him very clearly, and, well, one doesn't like to
stare. Rather tall——"

" Six feet ? "

" Oh, no. Just rather tall. Taller than I am, of
course. And he had a black moustache. That's
about all I can tell you."

The sergeant again consulted the sheet by his
side. Then he nodded.

" Yes—that sounds like the man," he remarked.
" Well ? And then ? "

" I had my dinner. And just as I'd finished the
maid came and said my visitor had arrived and was
waiting in my room. So I went up, expecting to see
the other man, but it wasn't, it was a different
man."

" Will you describe him ? "

" I'm just going to. He wasn't so tall. Rather—
stocky, you might say. Taller than me, though.
Rather, well, commonish. I think his hair was dark-
brown or black, but I'm not sure. I think so. And

something was wrong with his nose, it looked as if it had had a blow."

" Recently ? "

" No. I mean, it was sort of out of shape."

" Boxer's nose ? "

" Yes, that's it."

" Clothes ? "

" Yes."

" What ? "

" Eh ? Oh, of course. I'm afraid, I don't remember his clothes. I've not got a good memory, I don't often notice things—and then, at that time, there wasn't any special reason why I should notice anything, was there ? "

" You remember whether he was wearing an overcoat ? " pressed the sergeant.

" Yes, now you mention it, he was," answered Simon. " I think."

" Colour ? "

" Sort of check."

" You recall that ? "

" Yes."

" Then you must know he was wearing an overcoat, and not merely think it," the sergeant pointed out.

" Yes, so I must," agreed Simon, confronted with this evidence.

" And that's the lot—in so far as his description is concerned ? " asked the sergeant.

" I can't remember anything more," replied Simon. " Oh, large boots."

" Black or brown ? "

" Brown."

" Clean-shaven ? "

" Yes."

" Sort of bloke you might expect to meet on a race-course ? "

" Oh, yes ! Certainly ! Yes ! "

" That's three things more," said the sergeant grimly. " We find, Mr.—er—Smith, that people generally remember a darn sight more then they realise once they get their mind on to it. By the way, what made you think the other man was going to be your business caller, if you'd never met him ? "

Simon blinked.

" I haven't any idea," he answered, after a pause. " Now you mention it, I don't know. I just thought he might be."

" I see. Well ? You had your interview ? "

" Yes."

" What time would it have started ? "

" I think I remember that. Eight o'clock."

" Thank you. Eight o'clock."

" I think."

" Right. And now can you tell me anything about the interview ? "

Simon hesitated, then put a question of his own.

" Am I bound to ? " he inquired.

" No, you're not bound to," answered the sergeant. " You're not bound to tell me anything. But, naturally, in a serious case of this kind——"

" Yes, but our interview had nothing to do with that other man," interrupted Simon. He wanted to keep Mr. Mildenhall out of the matter, as well as Milly. " Nothing whatever. It was just a talk about our work, that's all. We—were carrying out instructions."

" Whose instructions ? "

"Eh? Well, Nugum Limited. My firm. Ours. Naturally."

"I see."

"And, of course, we're not supposed to talk about our business to other people."

"Well—the business all passed off quite normally?"

"Yes, certainly."

"And was just normal business?"

"Certainly. Yes."

Was it? Those envelopes? And his oath to Mr. Mildenhall? Yes, but why should he mention these things? They were private concerns, nothing to do with this police case . . . they couldn't have anything to do with it. . . .

"How long did the interview last?" asked the sergeant.

"About fifteen or twenty minutes," replied Simon.

The sergeant consulted his sheet, then nodded.

"Then he left you about 8.15 or 8.20?"

"That's right. P.M."

"Did you arrange any further meetings?"

"No."

"Do you know where he went?"

"No."

"No reference to his future plans or programme? No indication of his route? His next town? The next person he would be interviewing?"

"No. Absolutely nothing."

"Or where he came from?"

"No. Oh, but wait a moment. Yes, I can tell you something. Leicester and Nottingham. He must have been to those places, because he referred to business there. He mentioned Nottingham particu-

larly. He thought we could open a branch office
there. There's no harm, of course, in telling you
that."

He paused for a moment. The sergeant drummed
with his fingers on the desk. Then Simon went on,

" That's all I can tell you about him. For certain,
I mean. The maid saw him go."

" Yes, we got his description from the maid,"
answered the sergeant. " And also yours."

He continued to drum with his fingers, as though
he were waiting for something. Simon felt that the
sergeant was not satisfied with him. Suddenly he
recalled a point he had forgotten. The reference to
the maid reminded him.

" Oh, yes, there is something else," he exclaimed.
" I mean, something about his visit. He wasn't the
man who was first shown into my room. The first
man was—was the man in—in the cupboard."

The sergeant nodded.

" That is my information," he said shortly.
" Yes ? "

" Ah, then the maid will have told you about
that ? " asked Simon.

" She told the police at Brackham," the sergeant
corrected him.

" Yes, of course—and it's been passed on. The
whole thing is exceedingly—well, mysterious, Sergeant. I was quite fogged about it. You see—as I
expect she will have stated—she showed one man to
my room——"

" At about seven."

" Yes. While I was starting dinner. But she saw
another man go——"

" At about a quarter- or twenty-past eight."

" Yes."

" And she didn't see the second man arrive, or the first man go."

" No."

" Because—it appears—the first man didn't go."

" Er—no."

" Quite so. No. But he asked for you, you know, Mr. Smith."

" So I understand," answered Simon.

" Were you expecting two visitors ? "

" Indeed not ! And it wasn't till my conversation in the morning with the maid that I knew I had two."

" So you have no idea what the first man wanted to see you about ? "

" How could I have ? I only had that one glimpse of him I told you about, and I've no idea who he was."

The sergeant frowned heavily, rubbed his nose, and then said, in a tone both resigned and exasperated :

" Well, let's get back to the man you do know something about. There's another thing you haven't told me yet."

" What ? "

" His name ? "

" Oh ! So I haven't." Simon hesitated for an instant, wondering whether he were giving away a business secret, but he could find no reason for withholding it. " Raikes. Thomas Raikes."

" Ah ! Thank you." The name was written on the pad. " And now let me have the rest. What did you do after Mr. Thomas Raikes left you ? "

The first thing he had done had been to try to telephone to Mr. Mildenhall, but he did not want to

mention that. As the interview progressed, and as
he found himself already drifting into the confusion
of lies and omissions, his desire to connect up with
his employer, either telephonically or actually,
increased. Perhaps he ought to have known how to
act, but the fact remained that he did not, and he
longed for Mildenhall's further instructions. In the
absence of these instructions, he answered,

" I did one or two odds and ends, and then got to
bed."

" Your visitor, Mr. Raikes, left at about 8.15 or
8.20," remarked the sergeant, " so you got to bed
quite early, didn't you ? "

" Yes. I was tired."

" Do you remember what time you got into bed ? "

" Only roughly. Those odds and ends took a bit of
time. It might have been about nine, or a bit before,
or a bit after."

" Did you have any disturbance in the night ? "

" Yes, I'm going to tell you about that. I woke
up once and thought somebody was trying to get
into my room."

" Trying ? "

" Yes."

" Why should there have been any difficulty ? "

" Oh, I see. I'd locked my door."

" Is that your usual habit ? "

" Well, no."

" Why did you lock it that night ? "

" I can't say, exactly. I felt a bit anxious, somehow. I—perhaps I shouldn't say this, and please
don't exaggerate its importance—but I wasn't very
happy about Mr. Raikes."

" But he should have had no reason to come back,

should he ? " pressed the sergeant. " I don't suppose you were carrying the Crown Jewels with you ? "

" No, of course not," answered Simon, nervously irritated, " but I'm telling you what I felt, not why I felt it ! "

" Right, Mr. Smith. Go on. Someone tried to get in. What did you do ? "

" I went to the door and listened, and then unlocked and opened it. No one was there, but I thought I heard footsteps going away. Then I relocked the door and got back into bed. Oh, but wait a moment! I did something else first, and this *is* important. I—I tried the door of the cupboard——"

" The devil you did ! " exclaimed the sergeant, looking at him sharply.

" Yes, I'm telling you."

" Well ? "

" It was locked."

" Didn't you unlock it ? "

" I couldn't."

" You're not telling me it was locked on the inside ? "

" It might have been. I don't know. But it hadn't been locked when I went down to dinner, that I remember, because I looked in soon after I got into the room."

" Oh ! And was anything there ? "

" No. It was empty."

" Let's get all this straight, Mr. Smith," said the sergeant. " The cupboard was unlocked and empty at seven p.m. Is that correct ? "

" Yes."

" Key in it or not ? "

" The key was in it."

" Right. And when you went up to the room
after dinner, and found Mr. Raikes there, what about
the cupboard then ? "

" I can't say."

" You didn't notice it ? "

" No."

" Not even whether the key was still in it ? "

" I'm afraid not."

" That's a pity. So all we can say is that, at seven
p.m., when you went down to dinner, and before
either of your two visitors went up to your room, the
cupboard was empty, and the key was in it, and that
then we know nothing about it till you got out of
bed and found it locked and the key gone ? "

" That's right."

" What time did you get out of bed ? "

" I don't know."

" Didn't you look at your watch ? "

" No."

" Hear a clock chime, or anything ? Think hard.
This is important."

Simon thought hard and uselessly.

" I'm sorry, I've no idea of the time," he said.

" That's a pity again," answered the sergeant.
" Have you heard how long the man had been dead,
according to the doctor, when he was found ? "

" About twelve hours, wasn't it ? "

The sergeant looked at him curiously.

" Yes, about twelve hours. Or, rather a little over.
This means, you understand, that he probably died
somewhere between, say, seven and ten o'clock on
the night you occupied the room."

Simon nodded solemnly.

" Yes, I understand that."

" And that he was probably in the cupboard when you tried it."

" It would seem so."

" But, of course, a body can be killed in one place and then moved to another. Did you listen at the cupboard door ? "

" No. Yes. No. I may have done so."

" You were nervous ? "

" I don't think that was a thing to be ashamed of —under the circumstances."

The sergeant became human for a moment, and smiled.

" Nor do I, Mr. Smith," he said.

" Thank you," answered Simon. " As a matter of fact, I put a chair against the door before I got back into bed. I meant to ask the maid about it in the morning—I thought she might know—but when she told me about the two visitors—I've mentioned that, haven't I ?—really, I hardly know what I've mentioned and what I haven't—well, that so astonished me that it put the cupboard right out of my head."

" I should have thought it would have made you immediately think of the cupboard," commented the sergeant.

" I agree with you—now," replied Simon, " and it might have made any one else, but it didn't make me."

" Yes, all people don't act alike," admitted the sergeant.

" And then you must remember," added Simon, pressing his point home, " that I didn't know anything about the murder at that time, which makes a difference."

The sergeant drummed with his fingers again.

." Murder ? " he repeated. " Has any one suggested murder ? "

" Oh, I see ! You mean, it might have been
suicide ? " exclaimed Simon.

" Do you know how the man died ? "

" No, I've not heard that."

" Asphyxiation, due to strangulation."

" I say ! How awful ! "

" By the way, Mr. Smith," said the sergeant
casually, " how did you know the man had been
dead about twelve hours ? "

" Eh ? " Suddenly the sergeant swung round in
his chair, and faced him directly.

" In fact, Mr. Smith, how do you come to know
anything about this case at all ? "

For a moment Simon felt sick, and longed for the
floor to open and swallow him. He had heard of the
case through Milly, whose existence he had, by
implication, denied. If he introduced her name now
he would be asked why he had not done so before,
and why he had lied about the car. Suspicions
which he had been trying to allay would arise, to the
confusion of Milly as well as of himself. He would be
cross-examined more closely, not only about Milly,
but about Mildenhall. . . . And it would lead to
questions like this. . . . " Is it true, Mr. Smith,
that you went straight to bed after your visitor
left you ? " " I said I did one or two odds and
ends." " What were these odds and ends ? " " Oh
—well—as a matter of fact, I tried to telephone to
my employer." " Oh, you did ? Why ? And why
didn't you tell me that before ? " . . . Into the
imaginary cross-examination came the sergeant's
real voice :

" Well ? "

" It was on my way here," replied Simon, seizing on the first idea that came to him. " I overheard some people talking about it."

" Where ? "

On the point of saying " At an inn," he changed it to " At a station." Just in time he remembered he was supposed to be travelling by train.

The sergeant was silent for several seconds. Simon had a vague idea that his arrest might be imminent. The words "Detained on suspicion" came to him. . . . But all at once the sergeant rose, and exclaimed :

" Well, if that's all you can tell me, I won't keep you any longer."

Simon felt weak with relief.

" Where shall I find you if I want you ? " the sergeant added. " Are you staying here ? "

That wasn't quite so good.

" Yes, just for the night," Simon answered.

" Can I know your hotel ? The Dolphin ? "

" No, the Railway."

" Most of you fellers choose the Dolphin," said the sergeant. " And after that ? Where will you be to-morrow ? "

" To-morrow ? " Simon visualised his list. " Dill. The Three Balls."

" Dill. That's some distance." The sergeant wrote the addresses down. " Well, I'm much obliged to you, Mr. Smith. But I'm to inquire for you in the name of Grainger—is that right ? "

" Yes, quite right."

" Then if we want any further information, you'll be hearing from us. Meantime, I hope you'll get plenty of orders for your—what do you call it ? "

R.N.S. H

" Nugum."

" Nugum. I'll make a note of it. Oh, by the way, at which station did you hear about this affair ? "

" Eh ? " Simon thought swiftly, and decided on Chanton. He was quick enough to realise that he could not very well have heard about it at Brackham, and Bulchester was too close !

" Chanton," repeated the sergeant. " That's where you were last night ? "

" Yes."

" Why didn't you go to the Chanton police station ? "

" It was this morning," explained Simon, praying that the sergeant did not notice his collar was damp. " I was just about to enter my train."

" I see. And about what time would that have been ? "

" I—I can't say exactly. After breakfast I went to the station, and just took the next train."

" And had your breakfast early, I expect, to get in a good day's business, eh ? Eight o'clock or half-past, eh ? "

" Yes, round about that," murmured Simon. " And now, if you don't mind, I'd rather like to start my business."

" Yes, of course," answered the sergeant. " Well, thank you. Maybe we'll be meeting again some time."

With his head in a whirl, and guilt in his soul, Simon walked out of the police station. The sergeant looked after him dubiously.

" Now, is that chap a liar, or isn't he ? " he asked himself. Then he called to the constable in the hall, " Jones, bring me a railway time-table, will you ? "

CHAPTER TWELVE

CONFERENCE ON A GRASS PATCH

SIMON did not return direct to the Dolphin. Before rejoining Milly, he wanted to shake the dust of the police station completely from his feet, and he made his way leisurely to his own hotel, even stopping at a shop *en route*. This was for the benefit of any eyes that might be observing him. He wished those eyes, if they existed, to register him as a bona fide commercial traveller whose thoughts were solely concentrated on his normal business. At the hotel, which was up a hill next to the station, he made his usual inquiry for the room booked in the name of Grainger, and was shown up to a little room overlooking the station yard. It depressed him, but did not surprise him, to find the number " 6 " on the door.

" Has any message come for me ? " he asked, although it was early yet to expect one from Mr. Mildenhall.

He was told that none had arrived.

" Well, if one comes while I'm out," he said, " please take it very carefully, it'll be important, and say I'll be back here at—what's the time now ? " He looked at his watch. " Say, half-past one."

Alone in his room, he sat on the side of the narrow bed and tried to decide his next move. There was a smell of station smoke in the air, and outside his window a shunting train clanked dismally. The smoke got into his eyes, and the shunting sounds were soporific. His mind, tired and confused, began to drift into a static state. But all at once he jumped up from the bed and dived to the door. Milly had said that, if he did not return to her, she would go after him. He had been a long while away. Suppose she went after him to the police station, and introduced herself there as his chauffeuse ? It was this startling thought that sent him hurriedly out of the hotel and down the hill to the town.

He found Milly standing outside the Dolphin Hotel. The car was not visible, a fact for which he was grateful, and he deduced that she had garaged it. She smiled as he approached. If only life had been composed of nothing but Milly Brown !

" Get through it all right ? " she asked.

" Well—yes and no," he answered. " Is there anywhere we can talk without being disturbed ? "

She nodded, and led him into the front of the hotel and out at the back. Across a yard was a patch of grass and a seat. They sat down, and she said quietly,

" My guess is that you've made a mess of it."

" I have," he replied. " At least, I think I have, but I'm not sure."

" Describe the interview and I'll tell you. Though, of course," she added, " I'll only be able to if you don't leave anything out ! "

He endeavoured not to. He described the interview as completely as he could recall it, and she listened without a single interruption. When he had finished, she stared down at the grass, while he waited anxiously for her verdict.

" It seems to me, Mr. Smith," she said at last, " that you have made a thorough mess of it."

" Yes, but you don't know everything," he murmured.

" One day you may think it's time I *did* know everything," she retorted, " and meanwhile that sergeant knows considerably less than everything ! He doesn't even know about me."

" You know why that was."

" You don't want to drag me in. But—my dear man—as I've said before, I *am* in ! At first Mr. Mildenhall didn't know it, and now the sergeant doesn't know it. What's going to happen when they both learn ? Fireworks ! Do you really think you can keep me dark for ever ? I feel like a ghost waiting to solidify ! " Suddenly she burst out, " Yes, and as you're keeping me dark from everybody, you're keeping everything dark from *me* ! I'm not the police—though you told *them* more than you'd previously told me. I've said before that I don't want to pry into any secrets—you know that—but how *can* I help you, Mr. Smith, if I *don't* know everything ? "

Her face was flushed with momentary indignation. He knew that the indignation was solely in his interest. But she might have been indignant with equal logic in her own, and although he needed her help, it was to help her that he now decided to break his vow to Mr. Mildenhall, and to take her entirely into his confidence.

" You're right," he said. " I ought to have told you before. Here goes."

In her abrupt and unexpected victory, she wavered.

" Don't let me rush you," she answered. " Be quite sure."

" I am quite sure," he replied. " And one reason is that I want you to cut right out of the business, if you think you ought to."

Then he told her the lot.

Again she listened without interruption, and as before, when he had finished, she did not speak at once, but gazed contemplatively at the grass, digesting the new information. Her first comment was wrapped up in a question.

" And—after all this—what is your opinion of Mr. Mildenhall ? " she asked.

" White," he answered without hesitation.

" May I know your reasons, please, for still believing in his whiteness ? His Nugum, obviously, is a blind for something quite different ! "

" I've no particular reasons."

" Just intuition ? "

" Yes."

" That's supposed to be a woman's quality ! " she mentioned.

" Well, I expect men can have it, too," he responded. " Anyhow, I've got it about Mr. Mildenhall. And about one other person."

She did not ask him who that other person was, but a faint smile implied that she guessed.

" I hope you're right—about Mr. Mildenhall," she said. " Your opinions of the racy Mr. Raikes, and the vampy Miss Searle—who you didn't mention to the sergeant, I note—are not so complimentary ? "

" I should say not. And there wasn't any special reason for mentioning Miss Searle, was there ? "

" Perhaps not. But—let's work this out—Raikes killed the man in the cupboard——"

" We don't know that," he interrupted.

" No, we don't," she replied, " only when one man goes into a room and isn't seen to come out again, and another man goes into the room soon afterwards and spirits away the body—my dear Mr. Smith, it is as plain to me as my own little finger, and it must be as plain to that sergeant, if he believes what you've told him about it. Did he seem to ? "

" I don't know."

" There's no reason why he shouldn't, unless he catches you out in one of your little fibs ! Then, of course, it *may* be awkward ! But let's get back. We are assuming that Raikes murdered the man in the cupboard. Why he did it we don't know, but we can guess that he did it while you were at dinner, and that knowing you would soon come along, he quickly concealed his crime in the cupboard and pocketed the key. Probably he hoped you would be suspected —what's the matter ? "

" Wait a moment ! Something he said just before he left has just come into my mind ! " exclaimed Simon. " Something that seems to tie up to that, somehow."

" To what ? To your being suspected ? "

" Yes, though it was quite idiotic, and I'd no idea what he meant by it at the time. He said that I looked like the sort of chap who could go off the handle suddenly, and do something I'd be sorry for afterwards. He advised me to watch my solar plexus ! I remember his last words—' You look mild enough,' he said, ' but it's the mild ones who go off the handle, bing, just like that ! ' "

" I don't think Mr. Raikes's opinion of you would carry much weight with the police, if they ever asked for it," commented Milly, " and if that *was* his real opinion—which obviously it wasn't ! Probably it was just a little private ironical joke. He sounds like a cool customer."

" Yes, he was cool enough," agreed Simon, " although he got a bit nervy at the end, and wanted to be off with his instructions."

" Yes, what about those instructions ? " said Milly. " You've got four envelopes left, haven't you ? "

" Yes."

" In that black box I'm keeping for you ? " He nodded. " Ever thought of opening one ? "

" No, I'm not going to do that ! " he answered definitely.

" Why not ? "

" Well, in the first place, why ? "

" That's obvious, surely ? " she replied. " The contents might tell us something."

" And they might not," he pointed out, " and then what ? "

" We could stick the flap down again, I expect."

" Oh, no, we couldn't ! Those envelopes are heavily sealed, and the seal has initials on—H.M. If we broke the seal, there'd be no covering up what we'd done afterwards. I've broken enough of my oath as it is."

" In a good cause. So why not break a little more, in the same cause ? "

He shook his head.

" Look here—there's something you don't quite understand," he said. " Of course, I agree with you that Nugum isn't the whole of Mr. Mildenhall's business, but I'm still banking on it's being a *part* of it. I mean, I've got one order, and I hope to get some more, and the orders will have to be executed. By the end of this week, I want to be able to show him a clean enough sheet for him to make the job permanent, and—I may as well tell you, I've worked it all out—I'm going to let him know that I couldn't possibly have managed without you, and that I hope he'll be able to keep you on as well. That is, of course, if you want to be kept on."

She looked at him almost despairingly.

" How *can* you go on thinking of that kind of thing in the middle of *this* kind of thing ! " she exclaimed. " You're much too nice, Mr. Smith. Yes, of course I'd like to be kept on, only I don't expect there's much chance of it—or, to be quite frank, of your being kept on, either."

" Why not ? "

" Because—if you want it—I don't imagine Mr. Mildenhall will have any further need of you after this week. It's obvious to me, if it isn't to you, that you've been engaged for a definite purpose that has nothing whatever to do with gum, and that by Saturday that purpose will have been fulfilled—and that by Monday we'll both be out of work again."

" I don't agree ! "

" I know you don't. If you did, you'd take my advice and open one of those envelopes ! "

" All right ! Suppose I did ? I'm not going to, but suppose I did ? And then found out that everything was in order ? There'd be no concealing what I'd done, and I'd be in Mr. Mildenhall's bad books as well as the police's ! And what would happen then ? "

" What's going to happen *now* ? " retorted Milly doggedly. " And suppose you opened one of those envelopes and found that everything was *not* in order ? "

But Simon remained equally dogged.

" What's going to happen now is this," he said. " I'm going to have another shot at telephoning to Mr. Mildenhall ! I—I've simply *got* to get into touch with him somehow, and I'm not going to break my word to him until he gives me permission to."

" You've already broken your word to him, Mr. Smith," she pointed out, " by taking me into your confidence ! "

" Well, I'm not going to break it any more," he answered. " Is there a telephone in the hotel ? "

" Yes, but it looks rather a public one. I saw one person using it. The manager hands it to you across the counter, and then listens hard to all you say."

" Dash ! "

" There's a booth at the corner, though."

" Oh, good ! I'll go there. Will you wait here till I come back ? "

She nodded, and watched him quizzically as he leapt to his feet, nearly tripped, and hastened away. Then she took out her little note-book and wrote :

" Poor Mr. Smith ! Whenever he makes up his mind about anything he's over-emphatic to cover up his doubts, and he rushes off to do what he's decided before he can change his mind—or any one else can change it for him ! I wonder if I'm wise to stick to the idiot ? The trouble is that, behind it all, he's so horribly nice ! So much nicer, really, than most of the more efficient people I've met. I wonder what's going to be the end of this ? He must have boggled that interview with the police terribly. I wonder what they think of him ? Of course, he won't get on to Mildenhall, of that I'm perfectly convinced. In my opinion M. has done a bunk. What for ? Don't ask me ! But I've a wretched feeling that poor Mr. Smith is holding the baby.

" This is a nice spot. What a pity we're not here with all the circumstances different.

" There was something I meant to ask him, and forgot. What was it ? I started getting towards the point, and then we got switched on to something else. That's what happens with him. Jumps all over the place. Something we haven't discussed, or didn't finish. . . . Oh, yes, I remember. That woman. Edith Searle. She asked whether the first visitor, Thomas Raikes, sent any message to her. She expected a message from Thomas Raikes, who killed the unknown man in the cupboard. Because, of course, he must have killed him. What kind of a message did she expect to receive ? What is the connection between these two ? Is it a personal connection, or is it something that connects all the visitors ? ' Business representatives,' they're called. Business representative my hat ! Did she know what Raikes had done ? Why did she warn Mr. Smith ? Goodness, I'm getting quite like a detective. No, I'm not. I'm asking questions. Detectives answer them. . . .

" Here he comes back again. I can see he's had no luck by his face ! "

Simon's expression, as he returned, was eloquent of failure.

" I can't make it out," he muttered dismally.

" It's as if he'd shut up the flat and gone away."

" Perhaps he has," answered Milly.

" In that case, why ? " he demanded. " He seemed to attach such importance to my phoning him."

" I agree, it's queer," she nodded. " You'd have thought, if he'd known you couldn't phone him up, he'd have phoned *you* up, wouldn't you ? "

" Yes, and he may have ! " exclaimed Simon suddenly. " I wrote to him last night. Did I tell you ? I asked him to telephone to me, and there may be a message waiting at my hotel now ! "

" Then perhaps your next step should be to return to the hotel and find out ? "

" Yes, I'd better." He looked at his watch. " Will you wait here ? "

" Of course. And I've got a brainwave for the step after that, if there's no message—which there isn't likely to be."

" Why not ? "

" Well, if he isn't at home to receive a phone call, why should he be at home to receive a letter ? "

" That's true. What's your brainwave ? "

" We'll wait till we find out whether it's necessary. Meanwhile, since I'm not supposed to exist, I'll remain hidden on this secluded patch of grass, and shall hide in that patch of cow parsley over there if I see a policeman coming ! "

He was away this time for forty minutes. She filled in the period by ordering a snack lunch of bread and cheese and cider and eating it on the grass. She was finishing it when he reappeared. He looked gloomier than ever.

" Nothing ? " she asked, superfluously.

"Nothing," he answered. "So what's your brainwave? I'm afraid I haven't one."

"Then we'll have to adopt mine. It's simple and direct, and it kills two birds with one stone. I'll drive back to London and find out what the trouble is."

He stared at her in astonishment. The idea seemed completely fantastic. But when the plan began to percolate he saw its virtues, and he realised that the biggest argument against it was that he would once more lose Milly's companionship, and this time for a longer period.

"It's—a long way," he temporised.

"That doesn't worry me," she answered. "There doesn't seem any other means of getting into touch with Mildenhall."

"But if he's not at home, you won't get into touch with him."

"Then I'll have to get in touch with somebody else."

"Who?"

"How do I know? There may be somebody else at the flat, but if there isn't I'll get hold of somebody, somehow, and find out *something*!"

"Have you forgotten that he doesn't know of your existence?" Simon asked.

"No—that's the second bird my idea will kill," she answered. "You will write him a note explaining me."

He frowned. He was not good at writing notes. This would be even harder than his last.

"I think I ought to see him myself," he said. "What about our both going?"

"And what about Nugum, while we're both

gone ? Let alone the visitor you've got to receive
here to-night ? "

" Damn ! Dash ! Yes, of course. I've got to
stay. Only—well, here's another thing. How am I
going to manage another day without a car ? "

She laughed, but it was not only at the lameness
of the objection.

" Why, that's a third bird we'll kill ! " she exclaimed. " You're not supposed to *have* a car !
You're not supposed to have a chauffeur ! If I
stayed here I'd have to hide myself from that
sergeant, and I can hide myself much more usefully
on the road to London. You told the police you'd
arrived by train. Well, you can complete their
erroneous impression by leaving by train. And I'll
connect up with you at your next town to-morrow,
and we can pretend, if any questions are asked, that
you've just engaged me ! Where *is* the next place ? "

He drew the list from his pocket.

" Ford's Hotel, Welditch," he told her.

" Right ! " She wrote it in her note-book, adding
the shorthand memo : " And I hope he looks more
cheerful there than he does here ! " Then she said,
" And the next thing is, that note."

He could think of no more objections. And half
an hour later he watched her car growing smaller
and smaller on the road to London, and tried not to
feel smaller and smaller with it.

A voice at his elbow made him turn with a start.
He found the police sergeant at his side.

" Selling much Nugum ? " asked the sergeant.

CHAPTER THIRTEEN

THE THIRD CALLER

WITH a coolness that surprised him, for it did not reflect his true inner temperature, Simon answered the sergeant.

" Not yet," he said. " I'm just about to start the round."

" I see," nodded the sergeant. " Pleasure in the morning, work in the afternoon."

His eyes returned to the road for an instant. Milly's car was now a dissolving dot in the distance. Simon asked, to break a disturbing little silence,

" Have you found out anything more ? "

The sergeant's eyes returned to Simon's.

" We shall," he said. " We shall." Then he added abruptly, " Well, I must be moving," and walked away.

Simon had an unpleasant impression that the sergeant did not walk away very far, and although nothing occurred to corroborate the impression, he decided to give no cause for suspicion if he were being watched. Returning to his smoke-grimed hotel, to which he had already transferred his precious black box, he ordered a late lunch, ate it to an accompaniment of goods-train music, and then threw himself into his job with an assumption of care-free enthusiasm. One result of this pretence was that he did quite a lot of totally unexpected business, and it was ironical that his fictitious energy should produce successes which his normal behaviour had failed to secure. It was also ironical that his successes left him cold. He ought to have rejoiced. He ought to have purred with happiness. But Nugum now seemed as unreal as himself. The only realities for Simon were the mysteries surrounding it, and Milly Brown speeding on her way towards Mr. Mildenhall's flat.

He walked up the hill to the station hotel just after six. A sudden tiredness seized him, making his legs feel heavy, and the apprehensions he had thrust away began to return. The long shadows looked sinister. He found himself speculating over the few people he passed. Were they policemen in disguise, watching him? Was one of them Thomas Raikes, also watching him? Was another, lurking in a clump of bushes, the third visitor who was due to call that night, and who was having a preliminary squint at the new member of the firm? Eerie fancies accompanied him up the rising lane; and the dingily-rustic station, with its adjacent unprepossessing hotel, was an appropriate spot for their continuation.

Before entering the hotel he went on to the platform to study the time-table and decide on his train for the next morning. Something worried him as he took his list of towns from his pocket. "Dill," he murmured. But the list informed him that the next town was Welditch. "Yes, of course, Welditch," he corrected himself. "I remember telling Miss Brown it was Welditch. That's right. Ford's Hotel, Welditch."

And yet the name "Dill" stuck in his mind. He felt sure he had used it to someone. The Three Balls,

Dill. He could hear himself saying the words. But to whom . . . ?

Suddenly his collar became damp. A vision of the police station flashed into his mind. He had told the sergeant that his next town was Dill! He remembered now. Of course, it had been a mistake, but would that be the sergeant's belief if—or when—he found out?

He spent a tortured minute, wondering whether he should return to the police station and correct his error. He changed his mind half a dozen times, and in the end he found he could not face another official interview with the risk of making a greater mess of things than ever. Better let sleeping dogs lie!

A porter helped him work out the journey. It was one of those troublesome cross-country routes. The first train went at 10.14, and there were two changes. He would not reach Welditch till after lunch. That was a nuisance.

Leaving the platform, he entered the dingy hotel. It was dingier and more depressing than the hotel at Brackham, and the pale youth who appeared to be in charge seemed to be wondering, from his expression, whether to go on living or to commit suicide. If he were destined to go on living at the Railway Hotel, Bulchester, the alternative had points to commend it.

" Has there been any message for me ? " asked Simon.

The pale youth stopped thinking of death for a moment, and consulted a slate.

" Your name's Grainger, isn't it ? " he said.

" That's right," answered Simon.

" Room No. 6 ? "

" Yes."

" Well, I've a message," said the pale youth,
" only it's for Room No. 3." He peered at the slate
a little closer through steel-rimmed spectacles.
" ' Will Mrs. Cooper ring up Mr. Cooper ? ' Were you
told, by the way, that the only extras here are
baths, boots, lights, and service ? "

Then, looking unutterably bored, he concluded
his lukewarm interest in his guest, and returned to
his contemplation of the riddle of existence.

Simon went up the narrow stairs to his small
room over the station yard. As he washed, trucks
clanked below his window without appearing to
achieve any special object. He wondered whether
they would clank all night. He spent half an hour
on his lumpy bed, staring at the blackened ceiling.
The clanking continued, with short periods of rest.
At seven he descended to a gloomy dining-room,
and had a very badly-cooked meal. He lingered
over the meal merely to postpone returning to his
room, but he returned to it at last, and began making
a record of the afternoon's business. The trucks
went on clanking. He found himself getting jumpy,
and counting them. Then something else made
him jump. Somebody was knocking on his door.

" Eh ? Come in ! " he cried.

The pale-faced youth opened the door. He had not
left this world yet.

" Someone to see you," he said. " Will you go
down, or shall he come up ? "

" Please send him up," answered Simon.

The pale young man departed, and Simon returned suddenly to his papers. It would look well
if he were found busy. When another knock came,

he called, " Come in, come in," and did not look up immediately. When he did so, he found a tall, grave man, in a neat black suit, standing in the doorway.

" Mr. Grainger ? " inquired the visitor.

" Yes, that's right," answered Simon.

" My name is Rodent—Frederick Rodent," replied the visitor. " Of ' Ours.' Otherwise, Nugum Limited."

He smiled pleasantly, entered the room, and closed the door. His eyes wandered round the room with a sort of vague surprise. Simon tried not to feel ashamed of the room. He himself was also surprised, for his third caller had adopted the unusual procedure of announcing his name at the beginning instead of the end of the interview.

" No, it's not much of a room," said Simon, " but then my rooms have been engaged in advance for me." Should he have said that ? And, after all, why apologise ? If the choice had been Simon's, he would have asked for the cheapest room in the hotel, and probably got the one he had. The composure he was trying to reflect had been a little disturbed by Mr. Rodent's surprisingly respectable appearance and air of quiet authority. " Anyway, I thought it would be best for us to have our talk up here, where we should not be disturbed."

Mr. Rodent nodded, and looked towards the window.

" The sounds of those trucks might disturb some people," he commented, " but they shall not disturb us. May I sit down ? "

" Yes, of course ! " As Mr. Rodent's glance again wandered round the room, Simon realised that he

was on the only chair, and jumped up. " Sit here.
I'll squat on the bed."

Faintly protesting, Mr. Rodent took the vacated
seat, then bent and picked up a paper Simon had
dropped.

" You seem to have been busy," he remarked,
" and if you have secured many orders in this
unpromising district, I congratulate you."

" Thank you. I haven't done at all badly here,"
responded Simon. " How have you got on ? "

A tiny smile illuminated the corners of Mr.
Rodent's mouth, but he did not smile with any other
part of his face.

" Yes, let us get through our business first," he
said, " and then we can talk of other matters."

" Have we any other matters to talk about ? "
inquired Simon cautiously.

" I think so," nodded Mr. Rodent, " and I am not
referring to the weather. That is, the meteorological
weather. You say you have secured some orders
to-day ? "

" Yes, half-a-dozen. The names of the places are
on the paper you picked up just now. Would you
like to look at it ? "

He handed it back. Mr. Rodent digested the
contents unhurriedly.

" But I call that excellent, Mr. Grainger," he
commented, when he had finished. " Especially if
my information is correct that you are new to this
business—that you lack our experience."

" Well, I expect I do," admitted Simon.

" Of course, we have a good article," continued
Mr. Rodent. " There is no denying that. But—
gum ? With so many gums on the market, and such

little opportunity to make one variety stand out against another—the same difficulty obtains with ink—we have a difficult job. I myself have been combing Yorkshire. On the whole the results have been good, but I reported to Mr. Mildenhall that it would be waste of time to continue there—every industrial town has been covered, and for some reason for which I can offer no explanation, I can raise no interest in the coastal resorts. None at all. Have you any theory, by the way, about that ? "

" Eh ? I'm afraid not," answered Simon. " Unless, perhaps, sea air isn't good for gum ? "

Mr. Rodent's eyebrows went up, and all at once he laughed.

" But that is a most interesting theory ! " he exclaimed. " A new recruit with original ideas ! An acquisition ! Only, unfortunately, if damp sea air should, so to speak, invade the adhesive properties of ordinary gum, it should make room for something special that can withstand ozone. Nugum. Ozone-defeating. Eh ? I will put the idea up to Mr. Mildenhall. But meanwhile I have asked him to let me try North Wales, and I hope his instructions will permit this. I can speak Welsh, and understand the particular psychology of the people. I was brought up by a Welsh aunt."

" Really ? " murmured Simon.

After a little silence, Mr. Rodent asked, rather abruptly,

" Well, does that conclude this somewhat unusual form of business interview, or have you any particular points it is your duty to raise ? "

" No—I think that about covers everything,"

replied Simon, although he felt that so far they had covered nothing.

"You are sure ? Do not let me hurry you."

"Yes, I think so. I mean about the business. We've told each other how we've got on, and all that—and you've given your name——"

"Oh, by the way," interrupted Mr. Rodent, "it is spelt with an ' e.' But I hope that is my only resemblance to the creature the word alternatively designates."

"Well, naturally not. I mean, that is, of course. But you—er—mentioned some other matter, didn't you ? "

"I did, Mr. Grainger. And now let us come to it." He paused and stared at the bed post. The trucks clanked outside. "But let me begin with a question. Tell me, Mr. Grainger. You have been on the firm for, I think, three days. Is that correct ? "

"Yes, quite correct."

"And are you satisfied with the job ? "

The abruptness and directness of the question were disconcerting, but Simon evaded the thrust by asking back :

"Why shouldn't I be ? " And before Mr. Rodent could answer, he added, "Are you satisfied with yours ? "

"No," said Mr. Rodent bluntly. "Not in the least. If I may speak quite frankly, and if you will regard my frankness as no personal reflection upon yourself, I am not happy over certain members of our staff, or over certain recent departures in the normal mode of business. What is your opinion ? I am giving you mine. Do *you* consider our mode of business normal, and do *you* consider that Mr.

Mildenhall's selection of staff reflects the choice of a normal business man ? "

· " Well, I have no great experience—as you yourself have just mentioned," replied Simon uneasily, " but—it's true, some of the staff I have so far met have not been quite what I expected."

" I am sure they have not. Perhaps I myself am not quite what you expected ? "

" Come, I didn't say that ! "

" Or imply it," conceded Mr. Rodent, smiling generously. " But I shall not be hurt by your opinion of me, so long as it is an honest one."

Simon looked at his guest for a moment, trying vainly to read him. Reading people was not one of Simon's strong points.

" No, I didn't mean you," he said. " I was thinking of the others."

" The others," repeated Mr. Rodent. " May I know who they were ? " Simon hesitated. " Or has Mr. Mildenhall sworn you to secrecy ? "

" Well, you were talking just now about normal procedure," Simon answered, " and I'm not sure whether it's normal procedure for members of a staff to discuss each other."

" On the contrary, members of a staff always discuss each other," retorted Mr. Rodent. " They even discuss their employer. Particularly when they want to get into touch with him, and cannot."

" Eh ? "

" Haven't you found that out ? I have."

" What ! Have *you* tried to get into touch with Mr. Mildenhall ? " asked Simon.

" I have," nodded Mr. Rodent. " And for a very particular reason."

" What reason ? "

" You can't guess, Mr. Grainger ? "

" I don't know. Perhaps, and perhaps not."

" Well, what would you guess, if you had to try ? "

Simon could not think of a good response, so responded nothing. Mr. Rodent smiled grimly.

" Then I'll save you the trouble," he said. " I wanted to get into touch with Mr. Mildenhall to repeat an unpleasant rumour I've heard. A rumour that one of his employees is being suspected of murder."

Simon swallowed.

" You mean—me ? " he murmured.

" Are you suspected, Mr. Grainger ? "

" I don't think so. I don't know. But somebody else is."

" Who ? "

" Why, the—the man who called on me—on the night of the murder."

" Exactly. The member of the staff whom it is not business etiquette to discuss. It occurs to me, Mr. Grainger, if it does not to you, that we are beyond the rules of etiquette ! So whom do *you* suspect ? "

" Well, I don't really know anything about it—I mean, about who the murdered man is, or why it was done, but—well, who did it seems obvious."

" I agree, it seems obvious," replied Mr. Rodent. " So obvious that I cannot see why you think you may be suspected yourself ? "

" Did I say I thought that ? " blinked Simon.

" You said you did not know that you were not."

" Oh ! I see. Well—as it happened in my room,

as I expect you've heard—the police might think anything."

" The police. Yes, quite so. But they haven't been worrying you, have they ? "

" Er—no."

" They haven't interviewed you ? "

" Well, of course, I had to go to them when I heard about it, didn't I ? We thought—I thought it was the only thing to do."

Mr. Rodent nodded solemnly.

" I agree," he said. " And it must have been exceedingly awkward for you. What did you tell them ? "

" I told them—well, all I thought they ought to know," replied Simon.

" And—may I ask—did that include all *you* knew ? "

Simon flushed.

" You're not suggesting——" he began.

" That you killed the man in the cupboard ? " interrupted Mr. Rodent. " I doubt, Mr. Grainger, whether you could even kill a grasshopper." Simon wondered whether this were intended as a compliment. " Nevertheless, it seems possible—since even in this short time I have discovered you to be a man of considerable discretion—that there may have been certain business details which you thought unnecessary to pass on to the police. That was why I asked whether you told them *all* you knew ? "

" I see," blinked Simon. " Yes, exactly. Well, no, I didn't mention any unnecessary business details."

" That was wise—and, I am sure, in accordance

with what Mr. Mildenhall would have desired. The
more our firm can keep out of this unfortunate
matter, the better. I am only sorry, Mr. Grainger,
that you have not been able to keep out of it
yourself. Did you have any difficulty with the
police ? Were they quite pleasant ? "

"Yes—I think so."

"Although, I remember, you said a few moments
ago that they possibly suspected you."

"Did I ? Well, yes, possibly."

"I am afraid, Mr. Grainger," said Mr. Rodent,
after a little pause, "that it is more than possible."

"What do you mean ? " exclaimed Simon.

"When I came along, I overheard a policeman
making inquiries of a porter. I did not hear everything, but I have an impression—now—that the
inquiries referred to you."

Simon swallowed. He had told the sergeant that
he was going next to Dill. The porter would have
said that he was going to Welditch. Suddenly Mr.
Rodent asked bluntly :

"Would you like to cut right out of it ? "

"Eh ? How could I, even if I did ? " replied
Simon.

"I'm not sure. You're in a delicate position. I
have an idea at the back of my mind, but whether
it is feasible or not—whether worth discussing—will
depend on my next instructions. Have you brought
any from Mr. Mildenhall ? If so, perhaps I could
see them ? "

There was a naturalness in Mr. Rodent's methods
which contrasted refreshingly with the methods of
Simon's two previous callers. Mr. Rodent did not
create the impression of having an ulterior motive,

nor did he contort normal procedure. He had given
his name when he had entered, and he was now
asking for his instructions in a natural way and at an
appropriate moment in the interview. Responding
in kind, Simon found himself producing the envelope
from the black box as though no special significance
attached to the operation. . . . Perhaps, after all,
it did not ? . . . Perhaps a series of mere coincid-
ences. . . .

"I have never really understood," remarked Mr.
Rodent, as he took the envelope from Simon's hand,
"why Mr. Mildenhall goes in for these heavy seals ?
They look impressive—perhaps that is the reason ?"
He broke the seal. "Now, if he made sealing-
wax as well as gum, and this were his particular
brand——"

He paused abruptly, and glanced towards the
window. The trunks were clanking along their side-
line.

"Did you hear anything ?" he asked, lowering his
voice.

"No !" answered Simon, and followed his glance
towards the window. "That is, apart from those
trucks."

"Probably my imagination," said Mr. Rodent. "I
think I've still got that unpleasant policeman on my
mind."

Hastily relocking the box in a drawer, as though
it were incriminating, Simon darted to the window
and peered out. He did not see any figure in the
dimly-illuminated yard. When he turned back, Mr.
Rodent was reading a paper.

"Derbyshire," he murmured. "Beginning with
Buxton."

He finished reading the paper, then handed it to Simon. It was a typed letter, and it ran :

" Dear Mr. Rodent, I have received your letter and suggestion, but I doubt myself whether you will do much good in North Wales, or, for that matter, in Wales at all. I happen to know that a rival concern is pretty well established there, and after you have concluded your Yorkshire tour, and have met our Mr. Grainger, I would like you to comb Derbyshire, starting, I suggest, at Buxton. You will find the usual publicity matter enclosed herewith "—Mr. Rodent had the envelope in his hand, and held it up as Simon glanced at him—" and I would like you to make full use of it. Yours faithfully, H. M."

Simon read the letter through twice, surprised to find it as straightforward and as direct as **Mr.** Rodent himself, and handed it back solemnly.

" You will note," remarked Mr. Rodent, " that Mr. Mildenhall does not mention the name of the rival firm—another example of his business eccentricity. He should take us more into his confidence. However, that is perhaps beside the point. The point at this moment is that these instructions make my idea concerning yourself quite possible—provided, of course, you like the idea."

" What is the idea ? " inquired Simon.

" That, for a brief period, you and I change places," replied Mr. Rodent. " You go to Derbyshire, and I complete your own itinerary. In other words, we each carry on for the other."

" But why ? "

" To give you a chance of throwing the police off your track."

Simon frowned.

" I doubt whether that would be wise," he said. " I mean, it would look suspicious——"

" Not in the least," interrupted Mr. Rodent. " A mere business arrangement, which I should myself explain to any policeman who asked for the information. In fact, I would make myself responsible for the change of plan. Both to the police, should that arise, and to Mr. Mildenhall. Well—what do you think ? "

Simon shook his head, and wondered while he did so what Milly would think if she turned up with the car to find Mr. Rodent at Ford's Hotel, Welditch, instead of himself !

" I see you think *not*," smiled Mr. Rodent.

" No, though it's very nice of you to suggest it," answered Simon. " You see—well, the police mightn't be satisfied with your explanation to them."

" You can take it from me, they would be quite satisfied," Mr. Rodent assured him.

" No, they mightn't be," insisted Simon doggedly. " And then perhaps *you'd* be in the soup as well as me."

Mr. Rodent looked thoughtful. Then he smiled again.

" And now, Mr. Grainger," he suggested, " let me have your real reasons ? "

Simon smiled back.

" I'm not going to make any change in my instructions until Mr. Mildenhall himself gives me other instructions. I've taken on a job, and I want to see it through."

" That is commendable of you."

" Thank you."

" Even if, in these particular circumstances, it carries conscience a little too far."

" You may be right, but that's the only way I can see it, somehow."

" It is a pity Mr. Mildenhall did not pick all his staff with as much acumen as he picked you," commented Mr. Rodent rather dryly. " Only you haven't forgotten, have you, that all communication with Mr. Mildenhall seems to have ceased ? "

" That may be temporary," Simon pointed out.

" You still have some hope, then, of getting into touch with him ? "

" Yes."

Simon did not mention upon what particular method this hope was based. Perhaps, at this very moment, Milly was with him.

Suddenly Mr. Rodent rose from his chair and held out his hand.

" Well, in that case, there is no more to be said," he exclaimed. " We will continue in our respective capacities, and I wish you the best of luck. Tell Mr. Mildenhall, if you do get into touch with him, that I have tried to get in touch with him myself, and that I shall continue to do so from Derbyshire. If I am successful, I had better let you know. Your next is —where ? "

Simon hesitated.

" I—I'm not sure——" he began, but stopped short at Mr. Rodent's expression of astonishment. The expression beat him. " Welditch," he said, uneasily. " I don't suppose there's really any harm in letting you know that, except that Mr. Mildenhall was so insistent that—well—that I shouldn't talk about anything to anybody. I don't understand why."

" Nor, quite frankly, do I ! Especially if your interpretation of that instruction is correct, and the embargo is intended to apply to members of your own firm ! However, having risked telling me of your next town, do you care to continue the risk and let me know your hotel ? The one will not be of much use to me without the other ? "

" Ford's Hotel," answered Simon, unable to find a reason for withholding the name, and fighting depression.

" Thank you. Ford's Hotel. I will make a note of it. Meanwhile, I am glad to have had the privilege of meeting you, Mr. Grainger."

As though to emphasise this fact, he shook hands a second time, smiled, gave a tiny bow, and left the room.

CHAPTER FOURTEEN

INSPECTOR DAVIS read through the sergeant's report, aud then considered it for two minutes without speaking. The sergeant waited, concealing an inner anxiety, but the anxiety was alleviated by the inspector's first comment.

"Well, you seem to have covered everything," he said, "including Smith, alias Grainger, himself. What's your personal view about that fellow?"

"I'm not sure—it's hard to say," answered the sergeant. "He a queer cuss, but I thought he was O.K. till I began catching him out at his lies."

"And then?"

"You're in charge now, sir—you don't want *my* opinion."

"If I didn't, I wouldn't ask for it," retorted the inspector. "At the moment it's more useful than my own. If you had to bet, which way would you risk your money? There's nothing like the financial test when you want to find out what you believe."

The sergeant tried to speculate with a shilling in his mind, but remained dubious.

"Toss up, sir. Fifty-fifty," he said. "You'd think, on the face of it, that his visitor——"

"Raikes?"

"Yes. You'd think he was the chap we want, but in that case why was Grainger so secretive? Why

couldn't he speak the truth ? And when you catch a
person up in one lie, there's no knowing how many
others he's been telling."

" But as we know, as many lies are told to us
through folly as through criminality."

" That's true, sir. Only, well, there's lies and lies,
aren't there ? You've got White's report there of his
conversation with the porter. Grainger told me he
was going to Dill to-morrow by train, but he inquired
about the train for Welditch, and he's going on the
10.14."

" Before which I shall have seen him myself,
and shall be able to form my own opinion,"
replied Inspector Davis. " That may have been a
blind."

" *That* wouldn't let him off ! "

" Correct. It would imply a guilty conscience. Is
White a reliable man ? "

" First-rate. Remember Sam the Snatcher ? "
The inspector nodded. " He was on that job."

" And he's at the station now ? "

" Yes, sir. And won't leave till Grainger does."

The inspector glanced at some papers on the desk.

" I see he has sent in two reports so far. The first
about the train, and the second about someone else
who went into the hotel."

" That's right."

" Tall. Black suit. ' Only got a glimpse of him
as I was talking to the porter.' White hasn't reported
that this other man came out again ? "

" No, sir."

" Do you think he would ? If it were so ? "

" He'd report everything."

" In that case, the assumption is that our tall,
R.N.S.   K

black-suited man hasn't come out again, but is
spending the night there. It may not be important.
Now, here's another point. Grainger apparently
intends to leave by train, but you can't trace the
train he supposedly arrived by. You think he lied
about that ? "

" I feel sure of it."

" And that he actually arrived by car ? "

" That's my view."

" Based," said the inspector, once more referring
to the report, " on your little encounter with him
just after a girl drove off in a small dark-blue saloon.
Is that all the description you can give ? "

" I only got a glimpse of her, but she looked
damned attractive."

" I happened to be referring to the car."

" Oh ! " The sergeant's face fell a little. " I'm
afraid I wasn't quick enough to note the number or
make of the car."

" Too busy noting the make of the girl, eh ? That's
a pity. But you felt pretty certain he'd been speaking to her, and was watching her depart ? "

" That was my impression, sir."

" Impression, not conviction ? "

" As near t'other as dammit."

" And after that, White took on, and there was
nothing suspicious until the conversation with the
porter."

" That's right."

" There's mention here that he expected a message,
which he did not appear to get."

" White seemed pretty certain he didn't get it up
to the time of his last report. It was a phone
message."

" Which could easily have been simply a business message."

" Probably it was," agreed the sergeant, " but I was noting everything."

" Quite right. Better note too much than too little. Now then. Where are we ? Any nearer knowing who murdered who, and why ? "

" I'm not," admitted the sergeant.

" Well, I'm hoping you soon will be," answered the inspector, glancing towards the telephone. " You know, there's one point that seems to have missed more than one person, including the person most concerned—Mr. Smith, alias Grainger. The bag he left behind. He doesn't seem to have made any effort to regain it. Why not ? "

" Yes, that's rather odd," said the sergeant.

" Maybe he didn't want to reopen communication with an hotel of painful memories ! " observed the inspector. " Maybe, in the flurry of an interview with the police, he just forgot. From what I gather, and from what you have told me, he seems the sort of man who might forget things."

" There was nothing special in the bag, I understand."

" No. Just samples. But they gave us the name and address of his firm, and I've been trying to connect up with his Chief. So far, without luck."

" Is he away, then ? "

" Yes. His flat is empty. He usually lives there with his daughter. But she's away, too, and we haven't the present address of either of them. But I've a man covering that, and as soon as he gets any news——"

He stopped short. The telephone was ringing. He lifted the receiver, and suddenly, as he listened, his face grew grim.

" Wait a moment, Warren," he called. " We'll have the whole thing written down. . . . Get your pencil and paper, Sergeant. We know now who the murdered man is."

CHAPTER FIFTEEN

SIMON DOES A FLIT

SIMON got into bed unhappily. He was beginning to hate night-time, for instead of bringing him repose it developed disturbing thoughts and fancies on the black canvas of darkness. It also developed night-mares into realities. A body in a cupboard, if encountered at all, should remain a figment of one's brain, a thing to wake up from and laugh at ; but Simon had actually slept, so to speak, with a body in a cupboard. Moreover, the murderer had tried his door. . . . Suppose someone tried his door again to-night ? What, in the light of his new knowledge, would Simon feel like ?

But, of course, no one would get in. As before, the door would be found locked !

" At least, *did* I lock it ? " thought Simon suddenly.

He leapt out of bed and hastened to the door. Yes, he had locked it. He crept back to bed, annoyed with himself for having got out.

Clank-clank ! Dash those trucks ! Did they clank all night ? And, if so, why ? It seemed impossible that any useful object could be served by the ceaseless din. Probably they clanked just to annoy him, and to keep him awake. . . . Swish ! An express thundered by, seeming to aim direct at his solar plexus.

After a fretful hour he tried counting sheep. He

counted them as they went into a pen, till the pen turned into a cupboard. Then he tried doubling from one up to a million. But the police sergeant kept on correcting him, and calling him a liar. He tried making his mind a complete blank. A vamp in evening-dress and a solemn man in a black suit came and sat on either side of the blank. Clank-clank! Blank-blank! Clank-clank! The vamp dwindled and faded away. The man in the black suit augmented, till his face filled the whole Universe. Simon sat up, in a sweat.

He listened. Footsteps in the passage? He could not be sure.

"Yes, but Rodent was all *right*!" he reflected. "What am I worrying about him for?"

Not only was Rodent all right, but the envelopes were all right. They merely contained instructions, along the lines of the one Rodent had let him see, and publicity matter. And Rodent had discussed business sensibly, had shown himself intelligently aware of Mr. Mildenhall's eccentricities, and had behaved in a perfectly normal manner. Well, hadn't he? And hadn't he shown a kindly consideration, also? By suggesting that Simon went to Derbyshire, while he carried on for Simon? . . . Edith Searle had also suggested carrying on for Simon. . . . Clank-clank! Clank-clank! Clank-clank!

Simon got out of bed again and drank a glass of water. Then he returned, and tried a new device. He wondered why he had not thought of it before. He visualised Milly Brown. Immediately, comfort replaced anxiety. Her smile made a pleasant mist around his pillow. He was not sure that it should, but it did. He drifted into the pleasant mist. . . .

He woke up with a start. He could not determine the cause, for no echo of any noise identified it, nor was there any rearrangement of the dark scene on which he had closed his up-staring eyes—a black oblong of ceiling, its boundaries and itself invisible excepting at a spot near the window, where a vague slit of light emanated from a lamp in the station yard below. But he had a sense that something was happening, and the sense remained after the un-recollected aural summons had ceased. If, indeed, there had been any aural summons at all?

"Imagination!" he told himself.

The explanation did not satisfy him. The feeling of reality persisted. Suddenly, to dismiss a fantastic thought before it could torture him, he leapt out of bed, ran to a small cupboard, and flung open the door. By the faint glow of the station lamp below the window he discerned that the cupboard was blessedly empty. He closed the door, and sat down on the floor to recover the strength that had oozed out of his knees.

When the knees were in commission again, he rose and listened. From neither the door nor the window came any sound. He did not even hear the clanking of the trucks. He crept to the window, but just as he began to peer out he withdrew his head. A figure was in the yard below, looking up at the window. The figure's background was a wall of ghostly milk-cans.

"That chap's watching my window!" Simon reflected. "Why?"

The answer to that seemed easy. This was a policeman in plain clothes—either the policeman who had questioned the porter, or another. In any case, Simon's movements were being marked, and a hundred to one the man would board Simon's train in the morning and follow him to Welditch. And then what? Would Simon be able to shake the pursuer off before meeting Milly and learning what had happened in London? The last thing he desired was a further interview with the police before he received Milly's news and knew where he stood with his employer.

Then another question rose in his mind, and he had no answer whatever to this. The watcher below could not have awakened him merely by staring at his window! So—what *had* awakened him?

Before returning to bed, he went to the locked drawer in which he kept the black box, to satisfy himself that the box, with its remaining three sealed envelopes, was still there. He had been made aware of the innocuous contents of Mr. Rodent's envelope, and had actually seen and read Mr. Mildenhall's letter of instruction; if the other envelopes were similar, there was nothing especially significant about them. But he could not rid himself of an acute sense of responsibility in regard to their preservation, and it was with relief that he found everything intact. Then he got into bed, to turn and toss, and think and worry.

He only had one more spell of sleep that night, and it was short but by no means sweet. He woke from a nightmare in which he was chased into a railway compartment by the spying policeman and ruthlessly questioned. As he opened his eyes, a drop of perspiration slid down his forehead. He sat up.

" Can I stand much more of this? " he wondered.

Once more he left the bed, this time for a glass of

water. The washstand was by the window, and he could not resist another peep out. To his surprise, he found that the first greyness of dawn was mingling with the pale illumination of the station lamp below. The milk-cans were now more clearly defined. So was the silent watcher. Fatigue had evidently beaten him, for he had slid down to the ground, and was lying against one of the milk-cans. . . .

"Asleep!" murmured Simon.

And then came the mad idea which, later, he had such cause to regret. Why not take advantage of the man's slumber, and slip away before he woke?

The foolishness of the idea should have struck him at once, and probably it would have done so at another time and in another mood. But he was worn out and nervous, and the strain and confusion of the previous day had not been eased by a night of normal repose. Almost before he realised it, he was slipping out of his pyjamas and beginning to dress. Once having started, it did not occur to him to stop, and in less than five minutes he was fully clothed and had collected and packed his meagre belongings.

He did have one moment of doubt before he left the room. He stood quite still, a little astonished at himself. But he feared to develop the doubt, lest it sent him back to bed in a state of further indecision, and another glance out of the window showed that the policeman was still enjoying his blissful unconsciousness. He was in exactly the same position as before. So, tiptoeing into the passage, Simon crept softly down the stairs to the entrance floor. He did not have to trouble about his bill, for he had been requested to conform with the establishment's rule and pay in advance.

Now a difficulty presented itself. The front door
was locked, chained, and bolted, and the bolt was
stiff, and creaked. Suppose he woke somebody up ?
The proprietor inside, or the policeman out ? He
turned, and looked for another exit. Through the
dim grey light he discerned the back door at the end
of a narrow passage by the stairs. He made for it,
and found that the back door was merely locked.
One quiet turn of the key and it was open. He
slipped out, to receive a little shock.

The back door opened on to the station yard. Just
ahead of him were the milk-cans. Also the policeman. Simon's heart missed a beat, and the bag and
box he was hugging nearly fell from his hands. But
the policeman had not moved. As before, he sat on
the cold ground, his back against one of the cans, his
head lolling forward against his chest.

Behind the stacked cans was a track with a line
of silent trucks. Soon, when the light increased, and
movement replaced this uncanny stillness, the
trucks would begin their endless clanging again. . . .

Simon shuddered as he began to move away.

" That chap couldn't have been more motionless,"
he thought, " if he'd been dead ! "

CHAPTER SIXTEEN

WHEN A MAN has no plan he is at the mercy of the incidents around him, and the incident that shaped Simon Smith's immediate future, when he stood bewildered on the outskirts of the town, was a covered cart. The first indication of its approach was the mooing of a cow, and the gradual developing of the cart out of the dim light was therefore unexpected, for no cow followed. But as the cart reached the spot where Simon was standing, the cow mooed again, and he realised that it was a passenger.

The driver, an old man, glanced down from his seat and stopped.

" Wanna lif' ? " he asked.

This was so exactly what he wanted that, for a moment, Simon could not answer. That anything should happen right for him was unbelievable. But when the old fellow repeated the inquiry, he exclaimed, " Well, yes, as a matter of fact, I do ! " and then asked, as a sort of necessary afterthought, where the driver was going to.

" Storniwell," replied the driver.

" But how extraordinary ! " answered Simon. " That's my direction ! "

He did not know whether it was or wasn't, but when a man has burned his boats, he welcomes any direction that carries him away from the conflagration.

" Then coom oop aside me," said the driver, " an'
if ye feel 'ot breath on yer neck, 'twill on'y be Bess.
I'm takin' 'er to vet., see, the poor gall's ailin'."

The cow mooed mournful acquiescence as Simon
climbed up to the seat beside the driver.

The cart moved on again. For a little while there
was no further conversation. The driver seemed
content with silence, and Simon could not think of
anything to say. This was largely due to his fear of
saying the wrong thing. But presently, when the
last signs of the town were well behind them, and the
cart was lumbering along a deserted country road,
the driver remarked :

" Walkin' tour ? "

" No—yes ! " answered Simon. The correction
slipped out before he had formulated any reason
for it. Surely this old man was harmless enough ?
Lying was becoming a habit !

" I thowt you hikers carried yer luggage on yer
back ? " said the driver.

" Well, I get quite a lot of lifts," explained Simon
lamely.

" Oh ! I see. And do you always start as early
as this ? "

" Eh ? No. I—er—I thought to-day I'd like to
see the sunrise."

" Sunrise ? Well, she be risin' now. But I seen all
the sunrises I wanter ! "

Simon stared at the amber glow over a distant
hedge with feigned enthusiasm. The driver ran
on :

" Aye, and I'm not meanin' jest the farm work.
'Twas at sunrise my feyther died, so 'twas, aye, and
one time when we was all lookin' fer the blacksmith

'oo'd bin missin', 'twas at sunrise I found 'im in the pond. I reckoned it was suisside, but they brought it in a accident." He paused, and the sick cow mooed. " Mebbe 'tis better that way, but they won't be able to bring in no accident in that Brackham case. You can't lock yerself in a cupboard and choke yerself by accident, I reckon."⌐

Simon did not offer any comment. He continued to stare at the sun as though the spectacle absorbed him. Actually he was thinking, " Can't I *ever* get away from it ? "

" Though, mind you," continued the driver, morbidly pursuing his point, " *that* weren't suisside, neither. Mebbe we'll see in the mornin' papers that they've caught the feller they're after." He turned his head towards his passenger and winked. " And mebbe they'll find it's the wrong feller ! "

Further silence appearing unnatural, Simon murmured,

" Eh ? Wrong feller ? "

" Aye," nodded the driver. " There's two it might be. The commercial 'oo stayed there the night and left a brown bag be'ind, and the man 'oo called on 'im. I read the account last night to the missus. She thinks 'tis the one, and I think 'tis t'other. Aye, but what int'rested us most in last night's paper was the bit about the dead man's moustache."

" Moustache ? " exclaimed Simon.

" Aye."

" What about the moustache ? "

" Oh, didn't you read it ? "

" No."

" Mebbe you don't read them murder cases ? I can't say as I would, not left to meself like, but

the missus, she loves 'em, and so I ketched the
'abit."

" Yes, yes, but what about the moustache ? "
repeated Simon.

" Oh, I see. I ain't told yer," recalled the driver.
" 'Twas a false 'un."

" What ! "

" Aye, so it said. A false 'un. 'E was disguised
proper. So it said. And as there wasn't nothin' to
show 'oo 'e was, and 'e'd made 'iself up to look like
'e wasn't, no wunner they're still guessin' ! "

Simon's mind grappled with this new information
as the amber sun rose higher and the driver lapsed
into temporary silence. The man who had first
entered his room at the Brackham hotel had disguised himself for the visit. Was this so that Simon
would not recognise him, or so that Raikes should
not recognise him ? Which had he called to see ?
Could one be certain, indeed, that the man who had
been found in the cupboard *was* this particular
visitor ? Perhaps he was a third ! . . . Simon's
mind began to spin as new vistas of thought opened
the way to complete confusion.

The deserted road showed signs of waking up.
Smoke coiled from cottage chimneys. A little
traffic appeared along the way, and a car sounded
behind them in the distance.

" You ain't feelin' ill, sir ? " inquired the driver.

" Well—as a matter of fact, I don't feel too well,"
answered Simon. " Could I stretch out in the back
of the cart ? "

The driver looked rather surprised.

" Why, sure, sir—if you don't mind the cow ? " he
queried.

"No, no, that's all right," exclaimed Simon. "Don't stop—I can manage."

He scrambled into the covered back, and was lying on a patch of straw, when the car overtook and whizzed by them.

He had had two reasons for changing his spot. The first was that, seated beside the driver, he had been too conspicuous. The second was that, though he had nothing against the driver, who indeed was performing him a service, he preferred even an ailing cow's company. The cow could not talk.

The cart lumbered on. The cow, after looking slightly hurt at this unexpected human invasion, accepted the situation stoically, and resumed her momentarily interrupted occupation of thinking of nothing saving a vague physical discomfort. When the discomfort became less vague, it mooed. But after the first few minutes, Simon did not hear the mooing. Fatigue beat him, and he slept.

The sun was high when he woke up. The cart had stopped. The driver, turning in his seat, was peering at him.

"'Ere we be," he said.

"Eh? Where?" exclaimed Simon muzzily.

"Storniwell," replied the driver. "I don't go no farther." He added, as Simon's hand moved towards his pocket, "I never charge nothin', sir, for a lift."

Thanking him, Simon seized his bag and his box, and clambered out of the cart. The driver turned his horse up a side street, and a few moments later the horse's leisurely steps had faded away and Simon was alone again.

Across the road was a cheap eating-house. It reminded him that he had had no breakfast, and

that the meal was long overdue. He entered the shop,
and reinforced himself with eggs and bacon. Then
he went into a stationer's next door and bought a
map. His other map was with Milly in the car.

The map informed him that he was now farther
away from Welditch than he had been before he had
started. In fact, to complete the journey by train,
he would either have to return to Bulchester by
a branch line and then start again from there, or
get across country to another station some dozen
miles away where there seemed to be a direct connection. He decided on the latter plan. To return to
Bulchester was, in the circumstances, more than he
could face.

The next question was how to cover the dozen
miles to Ferriby Junction, which was the station he
had to make for. The obvious course was a car, but
when he inquired at a garage he found that the
dozen miles was stretched to fifteen, that the return
journey would also have to be paid for, that the
scale was one-and-three per mile, and the final
damage would be one pound seventeen shillings and
sixpence. A sum beyond contemplation !

He inquired about buses. There were not any.
So he decided to walk.

Simon's condition was never robust, and now it
was below normal. After the first mile his fatigue
reasserted itself, and each mile after that seemed
longer than the mile that preceded it. His legs ached
and his chest ached and his arms ached, and his
baggage grew heavier and heavier. Had he been on
the alleged walking tour, he would certainly have
carried his luggage on his back. Late in the afternoon he staggered into the station at Ferriby, and

sank down on a hard waiting-room seat to wait for his train.

He waited an hour, and then nearly missed the train through dozing. In the train he fought against the fuggy comfort of his corner, lest he should doze again and miss his station. Reaching Welditch in the gloaming, he alighted, and asked the way to Ford's Hotel.

" Ford's Hotel ? " repeated the porter, as though he were referring to something rather outrageous and not quite respectable. " That's at the other end of the town, that is. That's two miles away, that is."

The news jarred on Simon's nerves.

" It can't be two miles away, unless the town is two miles long," he retorted irritably.

" Well, the town *is* two miles long," said the porter, " and the station's at this end and Ford's is at the other. There's no more buses. Will you want a taxi ? "

This time he ignored expense and took a car. Welditch was a large, dreary place, but its size comforted him. He liked the sense that, if any eyes were searching for him, they would have considerable trouble in finding him in so large a town, particularly in this fading light. In a village he would have been spotted far more easily. He did not even complain when his taxi crossed streets with trolley-trams, disproving the accuracy of the porter's information, but the closed shops did give him a few conscience-twinges. He would be obtaining no orders for Nugum in Welditch, unless he delayed his departure in the morning. This Thursday, the fourth day of his engagement, would be a blank.

The taxi stopped outside a large building. Simon's mind was so weary and confused that he could never remember anything about the outside of the building afterwards saving that it was large, and that the word " Ford's " was over the entrance in dull gold letters. But he remembered the unusual size of the lobby inside, and the gold-rimmed spectacles of the man he spoke to regarding his room. Many other people were about, but none of them was Milly, and he was not interested in anybody else.

" Mr. Grainger ? Yes. Room No. 6."

Six ! Six ! The eternal Six . . . !

From the moving little throng in the lobby some-one darted forward.

" Six ? Room No. Six ? "

Simon found himself confronted by a pale-faced clergyman. His countenance did not reflect the serenity of religion. On the contrary, it was extremely agitated.

" A word with you ! " he went on, and turned to the spectacled clerk. " He will be back in a moment —I shall not keep him."

Seizing his arm, the agitated clergyman led Simon into a small ante-room off the lobby. It was un-occupied, and the clergyman closed the door.

" I have arrived early," said the clergyman, keeping his voice low. " Nugum. Kindly give me my instructions. We need waste no time. I have a— a pressing appointment."

The clergyman's eyes rested on the bag and the black box.

" Yes, but wait a moment ! " answered Simon.

" We cannot wait any moment ! " retorted the

clergyman; and as Simon's eyes glanced towards the box he added, " Are the—the instructions in there ? "

" Perhaps they are," replied Simon. " But this is much too—may I know your name ? "

" I will give you my name when you have given me my instructions ! " retorted the clergyman.

He dived suddenly for the box, but Simon was before him, and quickly snatched it from his reach. The clergyman's agitation grew.

" Don't be a fool ! " he exclaimed. " You shall not have my name until I have my instructions, oh, be sure of that ! Now, then, how much longer ? Time presses—yes, for both of us. You as well as me."

With his head in a whirl, Simon took the key from his pocket and opened the box. The clergyman watched him avidly. Simon lifted the fourth sealed envelope out, and closed the box. Before he knew it, the envelope was in the clergyman's hand. This time the clergyman had been too quick for Simon.

" The Reverend Armstrong Godwin," he whispered, with a humourless grin.

The next instant he had darted from the room.

Simon followed him, bewildered, ashamed, and indignant. He caught a glimpse of the clergyman flashing out of the hotel. Also of another figure flashing out after him. Yet the whole thing happened so quietly that no one else in the lobby appeared to notice it. Even the spectacled clerk did not look up from a book he was writing in.

A newsboy entered the lobby from the street. He had a bundle of evening papers, and was aproned in a poster. The poster said :

POLICEMAN MURDERED

AT

BULCHESTER   STATION

Simon fought sudden, intense dizziness. He visualised, through a suffocating mist, the man he had seen lying against the milk-cans. Then, through the same mist, he saw something else. Equally unbelievable. Milly's face.

" Come on," said Milly quietly.   " We'll get out of this."

CHAPTER SEVENTEEN

THE MAN IN THE CUPBOARD

MRS. MAYTON, of Five Mile Cottage—it was called Five Mile Cottage because it was alleged to be five miles from anywhere—asked no awkward questions. Ever since the fiasco of her own romance, the sole bright spot of which had been Mr. Mayton's sudden weariness of it and departure for fresh fields, she had lived in the romances of others, and she found this process infinitely more comforting and less risky. "They may be married, or they may be not," she thought, as she opened the door to the two motorists, "but do I care?" This lack of conventional caution was encouraged by the charm of the girl, and by the something-she-didn't-know-what of the man. Certainly he looked harmless enough; and certainly they both looked dog-tired.

Had she a room for the night? (Oh, then they *were* married, or ought to be!) That was to say, two rooms. (Oh, then, they were not married!) They had been going on to the next town, but as they were running out of petrol, and as their lights had revealed her sign, "Bed and Breakfast" . . .

"Yes, I have two rooms," answered Mrs. Mayton, interrupting what was, to her, a quite unnecessary explanation. "Nice rooms. Adjoining."

"And is there room for our car in your shed?" asked the girl, glancing towards an ancient erection next to the cottage.

" Yes, plenty," replied Mrs. Mayton. " I'll open the doors, and then you can drive the car in. There's some trunks you'll have to look out for."

Milly drove the car into the shed ; and a few minutes later they had been shown up to the two nice adjoining rooms—they were so adjoining that you had to go through one to get to the other—had deposited their modest luggage, and had descended to a back parlour to await a much-needed meal.

" Now, then—who begins ? " said Milly, as the door closed behind Mrs. Mayton's retreating form. " I expect we've each got a packet."

" You," answered Simon. " I want to hear about Mr. Mildenhall."

" Yes, but I want to hear about Mr. Simon Smith," replied Milly, " and why he turned up so late at his hotel this evening ? I was a bit late myself, but I was hanging around there for over two hours before he came ! And what happened at Bulchester after I left him ? And who did he see that night ? And who was the clergyman at Ford's Hotel, and why did he bunk ? And who was the man who bunked after him ? And why, when I came upon you staring at that poster," she concluded, her voice now very grave, " did you look like a ghost ? "

" Yes—I'll tell you," murmured Simon. But instead of beginning, he suddenly exclaimed, " How —how different it all is here ! "

" How different what is ? " she inquired.

" Everything. It's almost like, well, another world, if you know what I mean. Just the two of us, in this nice quiet room——"

" And a meal coming, and friendliness," she nodded. " Yes, I know what you mean."

" I wish—it could all be like this ! "

Weak sentiment was getting hold of him. " He wants that meal even more than I do," she thought. " I hope Mrs. What's-her-name won't be long." Aloud she answered:

" It will be presently. I mean, all these other troubles will pass. But, till they do, we've got to face them, haven't we ? "

" Oh, of course."

" Because that's the only way to tackle them. So, shoot, as the Americans say—in books and films, anyhow—and when I've heard your story, you shall hear mine."

He told it, beginning with his brief interview with the sergeant as she had driven away from Bulchester, and concluding with his almost equally brief interview with the agitated parson. He dwelt longest on the meeting with Frederick Rodent, and when he had finished she reverted immediately to this.

" You don't *really* believe he was genuine, do you ? " she demanded.

" Did I say I did ? " he answered.

" You rather implied it."

" Well, he certainly seemed more genuine than the others. And, as I told you, he let me read Mr. Mildenhall's letter to him."

" But you didn't see the publicity matter that was enclosed with it," she said.

" No. There wasn't any special reason why he should show me that," Simon replied.

" There may have been a special reason why he should *not* ! " she commented sceptically. " Why should an ordinary business letter and ordinary publicity matter be so heavily sealed ? "

" Mr. Rodent himself agreed it was ridiculous,"
he pointed out.

" Mr. Rodent, if my guess is right," she retorted,
" was the cleverest one you've met yet ! I'll bet he
was being subtle, and throwing dust in your eyes !
Why, even that letter might have been a fake. You
say it was typed ? "

" Yes."

" And signed, of course ? "

" Oh, yes. I saw the signature. At least, Mildenhall's initials."

" Did you recognise them ?   Do you know Mr.
Mildenhall's writing ? "

He shook his head.

" Listen, Mr. Smith," she went on, screwing up
her eyes as though to improve the focus of her
brain. " We *know* something funny—something
wrong—is going on. We *know* that most of these
so-called business representatives are not genuine,
whether Mr. Rodent is or not. Suppose Rodent isn't
genuine, too ? Suppose he knows more than you
think, or he suggests, and suppose—I'm just trying
to work things out as we go along—suppose he said
to himself, ' Yes, it's all very well, but those first
people have all the advantage, because at the
beginning Mr. Smith—or Grainger, whichever name
they know you by—will have no cause for suspicion.
But by this time he may be getting worried.' Yes,
he might think that, mightn't he, whether he knew
exactly what had happened or not ? So he goes on
saying to himself, ' Suppose he is growing suspicious ? Some of those others are mugs and
bunglers.' Yes, clever Mr. Rodent might think that.
' Well, I must jolly well see *I* don't bungle ! I must

act my part well, show no eagerness, and I'll even have a letter ready to show him, to put any suspicions at rest '——"

" Wait a moment ! " interrupted Simon.

" What ? " she asked.

" I'm thinking of something. Wait a moment ! " He cast his mind back. " Yes, now I remember it. After I'd handed him the envelope, and just before he opened it, he asked me whether I heard anything, and he looked towards the window. I looked towards it myself, though I hadn't heard anything, and then—feeling worried—I locked the box away."

" You mean, he took your mind off what he was doing ? "

" Yes. Either on purpose or not. And if it was on purpose, then it might have been to bring out—to substitute—that letter ! "

" I think you've got it," she nodded. " And, if you have—well, Mr. Rodent's innocence goes up in smoke ! It was a clever trick to put you off the scent ! " she added. " It's a good thing you did lock that box away ! "

" Whew ! " murmured Simon. " I—I must be green ! "

Milly refrained from replying, " You are—and that's one of the reasons you were selected for this job ! " Instead, she said :

" Well, you didn't fall for his other trick ! "

" What other trick ? "

" The same one that Marlene Dietrich tried on you."

" Marlene Dietrich ? "

" You know, that cinema vamp—Visitor No. Two. Trying to take on your job for you."

" Oh, I see. No, I didn't fall for that."

" So, after all, you're not so green ! Why do you suppose he made the suggestion ? "

" Why do you ? "

" Do you suppose it was to get hold of the rest of those envelopes ? "

" It might have been."

" I don't think there's any doubt, Mr. Smith," answered Milly. " They've all had a shot. Visitor No. One came back and tried to enter your room in the night, but you'd wisely locked the door. Visitor No. Two and Visitor No. Three suggested that you should quit and that they should carry on for you. Visitor No. Four—this evening's parson—didn't have time. He just snatched his envelope and bunked— with someone after him. And Visitors Nos. Five and Six are still to come." She paused, and frowned. " Do you know who was after the parson ? "

" It might have been a detective," Simon replied.

" That's my guess, too," said Milly. " In which case, we may have to thank the parson for having got the detective out of the way."

" Do you mean—he may have been watching for *me* ? " asked Simon.

" No use blinking facts, Mr. Smith. He probably was watching for you."

" But how would the police know the hotel ? " he demanded, after a moment's consideration. " They didn't learn it from me."

" That's true. And of course the porter at Bul- chester—the one the policeman spoke to—couldn't have told them, either. All he knew was that you'd inquired about the trains to Welditch. Still, the police have ways of finding out things—it's their job—and anyhow that was one reason why I lugged you off so quickly, and asked you not to talk in the car till I'd got us somewhere a long way off ! I was afraid that detective might return on the hunt ! . . . Let's get back to Bulchester for a minute, and to Mr. Rodent. When his attempt to take on your job failed, did *he* try to enter your room in the night ? "

Simon shook his head.

" Sure ? " she pressed.

" Well, not that I know of," he answered.

" But he—hung around."

" Hung around ? How do you know ? " he exclaimed.

" I don't know, but it's another of my guesses. Listen, Mr. Smith. You were being watched at the Railway Hotel, weren't you ? You saw the man from your window in the night. And that was why you left so early."

" Yes—I told you that."

" And you passed the detective on your way out of the station yard."

" Yes."

" And—it now appears—he was dead."

" Yes."

" And you didn't kill him."

" Good God, no ! "

" As you say, Good God, no ! But who did kill him ? "

" We don't know that."

" No, but we can go on guessing. Suppose Mr. Rodent *did* want to have another shot at getting the rest of those envelopes ? And suppose he *was* hanging around for that purpose ? And suppose, when he was about to start the job, the detective spotted him,

and there was a sudden flare-up ? Anything might
have happened—and we do know, from that
newspaper poster, that the policeman was killed. If
Mr. Rodent killed him, he certainly wouldn't stay
around after *that* ! And if he'd thought of trying to
connect up with you again at Welditch—you told
me he wangled the address from you—he'd also give
up *that* idea, wouldn't he ? "

Simon stared at her with both astonishment and
admiration. Before he could express either in words
the door opened, and Mrs. Mayton returned with a
tray. She made a special point of not knocking, but
was disappointed to find that the table was between
her guests, and that there was no evidence to suggest
that she had interrupted an amorous situation.

" Drink it while it's hot," she advised, as she set
two plates of soup before them, " and I'll bring the
rest in a minute."

When she had gone, Simon said glumly :

" I believe you're right. And, of course, my
slipping away like that has made it look as if——"
He stopped, not caring to finish the sentence. " Well,
anyway, you've had my story now, so can I have
yours ? "

" After our meal," replied Milly suddenly. " Let's
forget all this for a little while, and eat ! "

He glanced at her rather suspiciously. Something
in her attitude suggested that her news was going
to be no better than his, and that she was glad of an
excuse to postpone the telling of it. However, he fell
in with her suggestion, and for twenty minutes they
devoted themselves to the business of food. Both
needed it.

When the meal was over Mrs. Mayton, who had

punctuated it with many unnecessary visits, lingered while clearing away, but at last they got rid of her, and Simon, unable to curb his impatience any longer, exclaimed :

" *Now!* How did you find Mr. Mildenhall ? "

Milly took a deep breath, as though steeling herself for an unpleasant task, and then responded:

" I didn't find him."

" Oh ! Didn't you ? "

Simon's voice did not conceal his disappointment. Until communication was established with Mr. Mildenhall, there seemed no possible way out of the tangle.

" Then—we still don't know where he is ? " he went on, as Milly remained silent.

" Yes—I know where he is," she replied reluctantly. " At least, I know where he went."

" You do ? Where ? "

" He went to Brackham."

" What ! Mr. Mildenhall went to Brackham ! " exclaimed Simon in amazement.

" Yes."

" When ? "

" He—he seems to have followed you there."

" But what for ? "

" That will have to be another of our guesses."

" I don't understand ! " murmured Simon. " Do you mean he came on the first day ? In that case, why didn't he—— ? "

All at once he stopped, and gasped. He jumped up from his chair, and sat down again. He had to sit down again, because his legs felt too weak to support him.

" You—you don't mean—— ? " he whispered.

She nodded gravely.

" I'm afraid I do, Mr. Smith.   Take it as easy as you can. Mr. Mildenhall was the man who—was found in the cupboard."

Something happened inside Simon. It was something that had never happened inside that mild individual before. He was filled with a sudden, suffocating rage, and he saw red. Milly, watching him, knew it. She had never seen him so rigidly still, or with such a queer, repressed look in his eyes. For an instant he seemed like a different person.

But when he spoke, he spoke quietly, and her relief was great. She had feared that, in the reaction, he might go to pieces.

" Someone's going to pay for this," he said, " for there's one thing I'm certain of. Mr. Mildenhall was white."

" I think I agree with you," she answered. If she had not, she would not have said so at that moment. " But can I know what makes you so certain ? "

Simon gave a little shrug.

" I can't say. Just that one interview I had with him, I expect. Well, we're going on—we'll see this through. I mean, I will."

" ' We ' was right," she said.

" Thank you. But——"

" No ' buts ' ! I'm in this up to the hilt. If only you'd realised it, I've been in it, unextractably, if there's such a word, from the start."

" Yes, I suppose that's right."

" So, quite definitely, let it be ' we ' and ' us ' from now onwards. Is that agreed ? "

He nodded, and asked :

"Now please tell me. How did you find out? And what else did you find out?"

"Can I have a cigarette?"

He gave her one, and also lit one for himself. For a few moments she puffed in silence. In the next room, through the wall, they heard Mrs. Mayton's movements. Outside the cottage was the silence of night. Moving to a sofa against the wall farthest from Mrs. Mayton's, and inviting him to sit beside her, she commenced her story.

"I got into London late," she said. "Luck was against me again, and I got a burst tyre. Did I skid! And our spare wheel, I'd have you know, was useless. The result was that I ended the journey with my headlights on, and didn't reach Mr. Mildenhall's flat till close on midnight. And there, Mr. Smith, history seemed to be repeating itself. You remember there was a policeman outside the hotel at Brackham when I went back to it? Well, there was a policeman outside Mr. Mildenhall's flat. Obviously stationed there, on duty."

"What did you do?" he asked.

"Same as last time," she answered. "Went by. Then, after parking the car a little way off, I returned on foot. The policeman was still there. A man who was passing stopped, looked at the policeman, and I heard him asking, 'Any trouble inside?' 'What makes you think there is?' replied the policeman. 'Do you belong here?' 'Oh, no, but I just wondered,' said the man. I didn't hear the policeman's answer, but he got rid of him, and I felt that he'd get rid of me in the same way unless I proved I had any right to call. And, somehow, I didn't want to prove it just then."

" You mean, it might have been awkward ? "

" In the circumstances, it might have been very awkward. After all, it *was* a bit late for a female caller who wasn't too sure of her ground, with a bobby on the doorstep—wasn't it ? "

" Yes, it was," agreed Simon.

" I'm glad you think so, too," she smiled. " Don't run away with the notion that I'm one of these sure-fire people who are always on top of a situation and never make mistakes ! I was tired—but that's not an excuse—and my mind wasn't very clear. Perhaps I *should* have put a bold face on it and gone in then. But I didn't—and now I'm glad I didn't."

" I think you were quite right," said Simon.

" Thank you," replied Milly. " A spot of mutual encouragement always helps ! Instead of going in, I went away again, and spent the night at the nearest and cheapest hotel. And next morning— this morning, though it seems difficult to believe— I found out that the police had taken temporary possession of the flat because—well, they'd traced Mr. Mildenhall's movements, and knew he wouldn't ever be resuming possession himself."

" Traced his movements to Brackham, you mean ? "

" Yes."

" And also his reason for going there ? "

" No, not that."

" But what caused them to try and trace his movements at all ? " Simon asked.

" Your bag," answered Milly. " The one you left at the hotel. Some of the contents had his address on."

"I see," said Simon slowly. "They were really trying to trace *me*——"

"Through Mr. Mildenhall," she interposed. "And when they couldn't find Mr. Mildenhall, either, they made inquiries about him, too. His movements—on last Monday—were traced to St. Pancras Station; they found out where he'd booked his ticket to, and the rest was easy."

"Tell me something. The man in the cupboard was disguised. I mentioned that, didn't I?"

"Yes. You said that Rodent told you."

"That's right. Was Mr. Mildenhall disguised?"

"Not when he was travelling, I gather. At least, not when he got into the train at St. Pancras. But he was wearing the same suit that he was found in at Brackham."

"Not the one I saw him in earlier in the day? That was dark brown."

"This one was blue."

"Was he seen getting out of the train at Brackham?"

"No, but the man they found in the cupboard was seen—the man with the black moustache."

"Then—he must have disguised himself in the train."

"It looks like it."

"What I can't understand is why, if he came to see me, he should disguise himself!"

"There's a lot we can't understand," she answered, "but meanwhile all this doesn't help your position, Mr. Smith. I mean, their knowing that the man who was killed was your employer."

"Before we're finished they'll know I didn't kill him," replied Simon grimly, "because I'm going

to find out where the blackguard is myself! How
did you learn all these particulars, Miss Brown?"

"By pretending to be a journalist. There were
plenty of newspaper people around in the morning—
the whole affair had been kept pretty quiet until
then—and I managed to mingle among them. But I
haven't told you all the things I found out yet.
One was about Mr. Mildenhall's daughter—what's
the matter?"

"That photograph! Of course!" exclaimed
Simon. "I felt I recognised something about it.
She was his daughter!"

"Do you mean a photograph on the mantelpiece?"

"Yes! Why, have you seen it?"

"It was still there. I went into the room for a
short while. One of the reporters was well in with
the police—I think he'd helped them over another
case—and as I smiled on him very sweetly, he
wangled me in, too. Her name's Margaret, and she
seems to have left the flat rather abruptly, not to say
mysteriously, last Thursday. To-day's Thursday,
isn't it? Then it was just a week ago to-day."

"What do you mean, mysteriously?" he asked.

"I'll tell you. Most of this part came from the
lady who lives in the next flat. She said that
Margaret Mildenhall had arranged to drop in and see
her on Thursday evening, but she didn't turn up, so
she—this lady in the other flat, Mrs. Thomson, or
Tomkins, I forget which—anyhow, she called to
find out why, and said Mr. Mildenhall looked as pale
as a ghost when he opened the door to her. He
seemed confused, and told Mrs. Thomson, or Tomkins, that Margaret had been called away suddenly,

and wouldn't be back till the end of next week. That's this week. When she got back to her own flat she thought it all rather odd, and she wondered whether Mr. Mildenhall had been upset by a telephone message that had come through a little earlier. She heard his voice raised through the wall, and he seemed very excited, though she couldn't hear any words. Of course, what I'm now telling you is what she told the police."

"And what you got from the reporter?"

"That's right. She went away herself on the day after—the Friday—and only returned yesterday, so that was the last time she saw Mr. Mildenhall. Well, that's one thing. Now for another. Wait a moment."

She brought out her little note-book and consulted it.

"Yes, the next thing is this. Some papers—I don't know what papers—but some papers were found which suggested that Mr. Mildenhall had only been toying with the idea of trying to put Nugum on the market himself, and that originally he hadn't thought of doing so for at least a couple of months."

"Then what made him change his mind, and start the business so much earlier?" asked Simon.

"Exactly! That's what we want to know! And, also, how all these business representatives seem to have been doing business for Nugum Limited before it was started! The next thing is that they found a locked room which was evidently a sort of laboratory or workshop. That may or may not be important. My reporter friend thought it was."

She paused, and dropped her eyes again to her note-book.

" And that's all ? " asked Simon.

" No, there's one thing more," she answered, raising her eyes again to his. " And this interests *us* particularly. Though it didn't seem to interest the police. I found it in a waste-paper basket."

" What ? "

" This."

She opened her bag and brought out a torn post card. He stared at it in astonishment, before learning its significance.

" Do you mean—the police let you take it away ? " he exclaimed.

" No, I took it away without asking," she answered, " and it was very naughty of me."

" Mightn't it get you into trouble ? "

" It might—so now you and I are in the same boat, and must avoid the trouble by justifying all the foolish things we've done ! Because what I did was very foolish," she added, " and afterwards I was quite aghast at myself ! I acted on impulse, after I'd seen what was on the post card, and finding myself alone for an instant. Look ! "

She handed him the two pieces. It was a post card bearing an enormous figure 6, in the lower circle of which was written in small letters :

" Romeo & Juliet

II i

Line 85 "

" I bought a copy of *Romeo and Juliet* afterwards," said Milly, " and the 85th line of Act Two, Scene One, begins with a familiar quotation : ' What's in a name ? ' Well ? Does that convey anything to you ? "

He gazed at the words for several seconds before answering. Then he replied slowly :

" Yes. Quite a lot. I've heard four names so far, and two more—making six—are to come."

" And what we've got to discover," added Milly, " is what's *in* them ! "

CHAPTER EIGHTEEN

DAVIS ON THE WAR-PATH

INSPECTOR DAVIS looked grim, and the plain-clothes detective looked glum. For a few moments after the latter had finished his narration there was silence, saving for the ticking of the official clock. Then Davis said:

" And that's the lot ? "

" That's the lot," answered the detective.

" Not a clue ? Not a trace ? "

" Afraid not."

Davis made a little deprecating gesture.

" As a rule, Wilson, the police get too much blame," he commented, " but sometimes they get too much praise."

" And none's coming my way just now," replied Wilson, with a faint smile.

" So far, my lad, I'm not handing any bouquets out to anybody," said the inspector. " That goes for me, too. But—damn it ! You saw two men we're interested in—one, Smith, alias Grainger, and t'other an alleged parson who, as matters transpired, had called at Ford's Hotel to meet him. You chased the parson, whom we're least interested in, and he got away. Meanwhile, Smith, alias Grainger, whom we're most interested in, also got away. Now, speaking professionally, what would be your name for that sort of thing ? "

" A holy bungle," admitted Wilson, without hesitation.

" You've said it," agreed Davis. " Why, the parson probably did his bunk to leave the coast clear for Grainger, and you were caught by a child's trick like that ! "

" Begging your pardon, sir," answered Wilson, " that's not my view."

" What is your view ? "

" That the parson's flight was genuine. He was thinking of his own skin, nobody else's."

" What makes you think that ? "

" I may not be a hundred per cent man——"

" Bah ! None of us are ! "

" ——but I've got *some* judgment ! "

" All right. I'll accept your view. But the result is the same. Both have flown, and we haven't any idea where they've flown to. Nor do we know where to find two—no, three other people we'd like to meet."

" Who are they ? "

" One, Grainger's other visitor at Brackham. Two, Mildenhall's daughter—we've got to communicate with her, of course, but no one knows where she is, and assumedly she knows nothing about her father's death or we'd have heard from her. That's obvious, isn't it ? She'd come flying back from wherever she is."

" Well, it's in the papers now, so she's bound to read about it."

" You'd think so. Otherwise she's not due to return—according to what Mildenhall told Mrs. Thomas, the lady in the next flat—till the end of the week. Mrs. Thomas." He repeated the name thoughtfully, then shook his head. " No, she's all right. Just an ordinary, rather silly woman. Feel sure she's nothing to do with it."

"You mentioned three other people," Wilson reminded him.

"Yes, the third is that girl-journalist in London," replied Davis. "Can't trace her or anything like her in the whole of Fleet Street. She certainly isn't connected with the paper she mentioned."

"Probably a freelance."

"Out for what she could pick up?"

"Some of these journalists will sell their souls for a story."

"That's true. They lick Ananias hollow! But there's something else I haven't told you yet about that young lady. Sergeant Barrington saw a girl drive away from Grainger in a car at Bulchester, and from the descriptions of these two females, they seem to be the same person."

Wilson whistled.

"You agree that's interesting?" said the inspector.

"Very—if you're right," answered Wilson. "She went off to London and picked up a bit."

"And returned—where? Here? Welditch?"

Wilson looked a little uncomfortable.

"I didn't spot her," he murmured.

"Has she been described to you?" inquired Inspector Davis acidly.

"Eh? Well, no——"

"Then how the devil do you know you didn't see her?"

Wilson put up a weak defence.

"I said I didn't spot her," he pointed out, "not that I didn't see her. What's she like?"

"I'll wager she was too smart to let you see her, either," observed Davis. "Brown eyes. Brown hair. Good complexion—but they all have that these days. Intelligent expression. That's not so common. Height, about five foot four. Neat appearance. Attractive. Barrington's actual words were ' Damned attractive,' but for the official description I've left out the adjective. Blue dress. Small blue hat. Black shoes. All of which coincides with our London journalist, who adds a very clear voice and a quick, engaging smile to the list. Well ? Did you see, spot, or otherwise view her ? "

" No such luck," grinned Wilson.

" I didn't expect it," retorted Davis. " However, I'm told you play a good game of darts. . . . You know, this is a real puzzle, Wilson. And the murder of poor White makes me all the more determined to solve it."

" May I know what you think, sir ? " asked Wilson. " Is your bet Grainger ? "

Davis stared at his nails for a moment without replying. Then he exclaimed :

" Why the devil didn't I go to that railway hotel at once ? I got into Bulchester very late, you know—or, rather, very early in the morning—and it never occurred to me, after my chat with the sergeant there, that our man would do a sunrise-hop ! I wanted a bit of sleep, and White was covering the situation. I got to the station at seven—in response to their telephone call, after they'd found White's body."

" And Grainger had flown."

" He sure had. And I'm *still* waiting to see him, so can only judge him meanwhile by his description. Which doesn't sound in the least homicidal."

" You can't always judge by looks."

" Thanks for the information. If you want to know, my estimation of our Mr. Smith, alias Grainger, is that he is either a complete criminal or a complete fool. Nothing in between the two will fit."

" Suppose he's the fool," said Wilson. " Who killed White ? "

" I don't know. Possibly the same person who killed Mildenhall. A nasty bit of business with a boxer's nose. Or possibly a tall man in a black suit. That's not much of a description, but it's all we've got. It was poor White's own description. Yes, and that's another one we're after. By George, what a list ! Listen to this, Wilson ! Ex-boxer. Tall man in black suit. Parson. Smith, alias Grainger. His attractive lady friend. Miss Margaret Mildenhall. Half a dozen, and not a sign of any of 'em ! But.do you know, Wilson, I've got a hunch that it'll be an even bigger list before we're through, and that we haven't yet met the one who ought to head the list ! "

" You mean the old stuff ? " queried Wilson. " Criminal gang, with a master mind or hidden hand that keeps well in the background ? "

" Something of the sort."

" Why shouldn't Mildenhall himself be at the head of the list ? " suggested Wilson.

" Why not ? " answered Davis. " Or his daughter? Or Smith, alias Grainger ? Anyway, we've got to catch Grainger, and since no one else seems able to do it, I'm now taking on that little job myself ! "

" Good luck to you, sir," smiled Wilson. " May I know where you're going to look for him ? "

" Well, I'm going to take a pot shot and try the Three Balls, at Dill. That's where he told Sergeant

Barrington he was going, and he hasn't been there yet."

" Is it likely he'll go where he said he would ? "

" Not in the least. That's why I think it rather a good idea."

Wilson shook his head dubiously.

" There's probably no such place," he commented.

" On the contrary, there is such a place," retorted the inspector, " and about a week ago a room was booked there for a man named Grainger. Room No. Six."

CHAPTER NINETEEN

THE ETERNAL SIX

MRS. MAYTON did not get much company, and when
it came her way she liked to benefit by it. Thus it
fell that, after she had cleared away and washed up
the supper things, fixed the coke boiler, turned the
beds down, smoked the clay pipe that was her secret
vice, and read a chapter of the Bible, which she did
every evening just in case, she decided that she had
given her visitors quite long enough by themselves,
and entered the parlour. Again entering without
knocking, she was again disappointed in finding no
evidences of romance.

" I hope you don't mind my doing a little bit of
sewing in here, do you ? " she breathed, clearly
intending to do the sewing whether they minded or
not. " There's only the one sitting-room, and my
visitors never make any objections. It's nice to have
a little bit of a chat, I always think, before going to
bed."

This unwelcome intrusion ended, for the time
being, conversation on important matters, and for a
while Simon and Milly had to endure Mrs. Mayton's
views and opinions on trivial concerns. They did
their best to show polite interest, and they waited
patiently for her to go. Unfortunately, she showed
not the slightest disposition to go, and passed from
the weather to the skirt she was altering, and from
the skirt to the disappointing fruit prospects, and

from the fruit prospects to a niece's wedding she had attended a month previously.

" She looked ever so pretty," she said. " There, that's her on the mantelpiece, just coming out of the church."

They turned their heads obediently towards the mantelpiece, and offered insincere compliments.

" He's in the police force."

They tried to be impressed by this fact.

" Of course, they were both very young to marry, but there, when two young people are head over heels in love with each other, what are you to do ? "

They hadn't any idea.

" What *I* always say," went on Mrs. Mayton, " is that love is nobody's business but those concerned. We've all got our faults, who hasn't, but that's one thing about me, I'm not interfering. No, that's one of the things I won't stand for. Interfering."

They murmured their admiration of this broad-minded attitude.

" Yet there's some who are never satisfied without they've got their finger in somebody else's pie. I had an uncle—he died last Christmas, that's him up on the wall—everybody looked up to him, and so did I, bar that one thing. Why, there was once, I remember . . ."

She ran on steadily for ten minutes more, then suddenly stopped.

" I caught you that time ! Yawning ! " she exclaimed. " You're tired, the pair of you. Why don't you go up to bed ? "

It seemed a good idea, since Mrs. Mayton herself showed no sign of putting it into execution. Milly jumped up, grateful for the excuse. Good-nights were exchanged, and the released captives left the oppressive parlour and ascended to the bedroom floor. At the single entrance to their adjoining rooms, Milly suddenly paused and giggled.

"Fancy! Only last Monday you and I were thinking of Mrs. Grundy!"

Simon flushed slightly.

"We can't help it, can we?" he said.

"No, we can't help it," she smiled, and went in.

The inner room was hers, but she paused half-way across the floor and laughed again. Some imp seemed to have got inside her.

"You make it a habit to lock your door to the passage, don't you?" she asked.

"Er—yes," he answered. "Up to now."

"Well, you needn't break the habit just because I'll be on the inside of it."

"Thank you. But, of course, you'll lock your door, too."

"Why should I?" she retorted. "You lock yours because you don't trust what's outside. But I trust what's outside mine. Besides, it'll give me a comforting feeling to know I can rush in to you at once in an emergency. What *I'm* going to lock is my window!"

Then she continued on her way to her room, but called over her shoulder as she passed in:

"Don't get to bed just yet, please. We haven't really settled anything yet, and we've a lot more to talk about."

She closed the door behind her, and Simon sat on the edge of his bed to await her return. Since he was not to start getting undressed, there was nothing to do but to ponder, for on his previous visit to the room he had performed his very mild unpacking and locked away the black box in the bottom drawer of a shabby wardrobe. He thought of Mr. Mildenhall, and found he could not do so without an odd pain in his heart. " Why do I worry about him like this ? " he asked himself. " He's nothing to me ! Why, I never knew of his existence a week ago." Neither, for that matter, had he known of the existence of Milly Brown. " He may be a rogue. And look what a pickle he's got me into ! " But he went on worrying, just the same, and he knew that he was trying to destroy the pain with false arguments. He knew, though he could not say why, that Henry Mildenhall was not a rogue. He knew that his first favourable impression of that unfortunate man was correct, and that his death had ended an association that might have developed into something greatly worth while. And he knew that he would not be satisfied until he had done all he humanly could to bring Mildenhall's murderer to justice.

Why had Mildenhall disguised himself and followed Simon to Brackham ? Had that been his original intention, or had something new developed that made another meeting necessary ? Simon strove hard to answer this question, but the answer remained a blank, as did the answers to many other questions he was determined to solve. . . .

He looked up suddenly. Milly was standing before him. For a moment he forgot all about Mildenhall, for this was a new Milly—one he had sensed, but had not expected to see. She was no longer in the blue coat and skirt and black shoes in which he had always seen her, and which formed a part of her official description. She was wearing a blue dressing-gown and bedroom slippers. He exaggerated the change into an unexpected compliment, and fought against a ridiculous embarrassment.

" I thought I'd make myself comfortable," she remarked casually. " Do you mind ? "

" Of course not ! " he exclaimed ; and, jumping up, pushed an arm-chair from one position to another.

The first position of the chair had been perfectly adequate.

She sat down, and he returned to the edge of the bed. There was another chair, but he wanted to remain mobile. From the edge of the bed he could get up and walk about, should this distracting vision interfere with his clear thinking, as it was very likely to do if he had it constantly before him.

" Well ? Have you got anywhere ? " she asked.

" No, not yet," he answered.

" Good ! If you had, you'd have left me behind," she responded, " because so far I haven't got anywhere, either. Now we can go on exploring together. . . . I say, Mr. Smith ! "

" What ? "

" Haven't you *ever* seen a lady in a dressing-gown before ? "

" I'm sorry."

" You needn't be. It's only my fun. Let's remember a sun's still shining in the sky while groping through this murky darkness ! Now, then, where shall we begin ? From where we left off ? "

He wrenched his mind back to business.

" We were talking about those names when Mrs. Mayton barged in on us," he answered.

" That's right," she nodded. " We were wondering what they meant—because they obviously mean something."

"Yes, that's obvious," he agreed: "And, what's more, something that Mr. Mildenhall wanted to know himself pretty badly."

"What makes you think that?"

"Well, didn't he tell me to phone up the names each night? And haven't I been trying to?"

"I believe we're getting somewhere now," she said. "Even if it isn't very far. Mildenhall needed those names, and he gave the envelopes—through you—in exchange for them. Mr. Smith! *What's* in those envelopes?"

"It—would be interesting to know."

"I've said so all along! And I do think that now is the moment to satisfy our curiosity!"

He glanced towards the wardrobe drawer.

"Come along! You've got two left!" she urged. "Let's open one of them."

But still he hesitated.

"We could never do it without breaking the seal," he murmured.

"Then, my dear man, let's *break* the seal!"

"And show we've tampered with it?"

"Would that matter?"

"I believe it might. You see——" He paused, thinking hard. "Yes, you see, it seems to me that we've got to get hold of those last two names—to complete the six of them—and will we be able to do so if we——"

"Mess up our bait?" she finished for him. "Something in that, Mr. Smith. If the envelopes have been opened, they'll smell a rat and get coy. Or —ugly."

R.N.S.   N

" I'm glad you see my point," he replied.

" I see it, but do I agree with it ? I'm not sure. After all, what are we going to do with the six names when we've got them ? "

" We don't know yet. We may then."

" And meanwhile, do we keep our incomplete knowledge from the police ? "

" Yes," he answered emphatically.

" You don't think we ought to throw in our hand, then, and go to them ? " she asked.

" Do you ? "

" It was my question."

" All right, then. I don't ! And I'll tell you why." Now he jumped up from the bed, and stood before her. " Listen, Miss Brown. I've been a mug, and I've got us both in a mess, but as far as I can see the only way out of the mess is to go through with it, and to pay our next call on the police when we've got something to show them."

" Always providing they don't call on us first," she said. " We could show them something now."

" What ? "

" Well, my torn post card, to begin with."

" Will that help them ? "

" It will put them on the track of those names——"

" But we're already on the track," he interposed, " and if we play our cards cleverly, we can get to the end of the track—which the police can't ! I mean, I'm the only one who can carry the game on."

" Yes, I see what you mean. And the police may bungle it."

" Well, mightn't they ? I mean, this particular clue. I believe we can help them best by following

up this clue ourselves, while they're following up all
the others. And what I've got to do now—wait a
moment—let's think—yes, what I've got to do now
is to act as though I were as crooked as they are,
to keep their suspicions down. . . . Wait a moment,
wait a moment ! "

He began pacing up and down, and she watched
him curiously. Suddenly he stopped before her
again, his face flushed.

" I say ! "

" What ? "

" Suppose—suppose I could work things so that
we not only got the six names, and found out what
they meant, but I collected the six people themselves—at the last hotel, eh ?—and handed the
whole bagful over ! By God, I'd like to ! "

He ran to the wardrobe drawer, stooped, and
unlocked it. He took out the black box and unlocked that. Then he extracted the two remaining
letters and stared at the heavy seals.

" Shall we try and open one without breaking
the seal ? " she asked.

" It looks impossible," he muttered.

He moved back to her, and she took one of the
envelopes from him. The seal was a perfect oval of
hardened red wax, its smooth ramparts, a quarter
of an inch high, enclosing the initials " H.M.,"
stamped by a signet ring.

" We might soften it with a match," she suggested.

" Even if we could, we'd never get it to look the
same again. And look at the flap. Every bit of it's
stuck securely. We'd have to tear that."

" We could use another envelope afterwards."

" By Jove—that's true ! " But a moment later

he shook his head. " No, I believe they might smell a rat. I believe they've been told they'll receive sealed envelopes, and that they'll be suspicious of anything else. They're probably getting suspicious already, and if I don't connect up with the last two, my whole plan falls to the ground. And besides," he added, " is it so important, after all, that we see what's in these envelopes ? Can't we guess ? "

She nodded.

" All but the amount ! "

" Exactly ! And how is it going to help us, if we know whether the amount is five pounds or fifty ? "

" It's more than five pounds," she answered, feeling the envelope's bulk. " It may be more than fifty."

" Say it's fifty. Six times that is three hundred. Mildenhall was paying three hundred for these six names. They must be pretty important ! . . . The four we've got so far are Raikes, Searle, Rodent, and Godwin——"

" How do you spell the first two ? " she interposed.

" Eh ? "

" R-a-k-e-s and S-e-r-l-e ? "

" No," he recalled. " R-a-i-k-e-s and S-e-a-r-l-e."

" How do you know ? "

" They told me."

" Suggesting they knew that the spelling was important ! Has it struck you, Mr. Smith, that each of those four names contains six letters ? "

" Good Lord ! " he murmured. " So they do ! "

CHAPTER TWENTY

PLAN OF CAMPAIGN

ONE MORE point had to be settled before they went to bed. So far they had not decided on the morrow's programme.

"What are you going to do?" asked Milly. "Do I drive you to Dill, and do you still canvass the town for orders?"

"No, I don't think so," he answered, after a moment's reflection. "It seems rather useless now, somehow."

"I agree.. If the death of your Chief doesn't cancel Nugum Limited, at least it suspends its activities! That's to say," she corrected herself, "the strictly business activities."

"And there's another reason why I don't want to go to Dill until I have to," said Simon.

"The police?"

He nodded.

"You're right," she agreed. "The police have missed you here, but they may try their luck at Dill. It's a pity you mentioned the actual hotel to that sergeant at Bulchester."

"But, after all," he answered, "is there much chance of the police expecting me there? They think I lied to them—I mean, deliberately—and so they'd think I had no intention of going to Dill at all. They may even believe I made up the name of the hotel."

" They may," she replied, " and they probably did. But what would they do, in that case ? "

" What ? "

" Wouldn't they check up the name ? And when they found there *was* a Three Balls at Dill, wouldn't they sit up and take notice ? And wouldn't they perhaps inquire about a Mr. Grainger, and find out that you'd booked a room there, not for to-night, as stated, but for to-morrow night, as not stated ? "

" Whew ! " murmured Simon, awed by this piece of accurate divination. " Yes ! I say, I've got to be careful ! "

" You have ! I think we stay tucked away in this cottage all of to-morrow, right until the train starts."

" Eh ? Train ? "

" Metaphor, my dear man. Actually, until our car starts. If we decide to start it. Let's talk about that. Do we go by the car, or don't we ? This car's been seen about a bit ! "

" Yes, they may know it ! "

" That's what I'm thinking. They probably do, and are looking out for it. And—it's Mildenhall's car."

They spent several minutes trying to discover an alternative method of travelling but could not find one that was practicable.

" Afraid we'll have to use the car, Mr. Smith," she sighed. " We daren't leave ourselves without it. Luckily it will be dark, and perhaps I can dim the tail-light, and fix something careless-like over a part of the number."

" That might get us pulled up on the road," he pointed out.

" Not if I did it very careful careless-like. However, we'll see. . . . Oh, damn ! "

" What ? "

" Probably it *won't* be dark when we start ! How far is Dill ? Have you worked it out ? The map's in the car. Don't get it—you'll bump into Mrs. Mayton, and she'll keep you for ages ! "

" I don't need to get it," he responded. " I had to buy another map when you were in London, and here it is." He produced it, and they studied it together. Dill was about fifty miles away.

" Not so bad," she commented. " I can do it in an hour. What time do your visitors generally turn up ? "

" About eightish," he told her.

" I'd like not to leave here till seven. I expect your guests would always wait if we were late, wouldn't they ? "

" I don't think there's much doubt about that ! "

" So we needn't worry that we'll miss Guest No. 5 at the Three Balls if we aren't quite punctual. The Three Balls ! What a name ! Now, then, where are we ? We've decided that Guest No. 5 will wait for you, but suppose a policeman is waiting for you, too ? What happens then ? "

" I'll have to dodge him somehow," he answered.

" How ? Somehow's no good ! " she retorted. " Wait a bit ! I'm getting an idea. No, I'm not— yes, I am ! Listen ! I don't drive you to the hotel, but to some spot nearby——"

" Well, of course," he interposed. " That's my idea, too."

" Yes, but I haven't finished. I suppose your idea was that I should wait for you in the car ? "

" Yes."

" Mine is that *you* wait for *me* in the car ! I go to
the hotel myself, and let you know if a policeman
is there."

" You've forgotten something."

" What ? "

" Why, that the policeman will probably be looking for you, too."

" No, I've not forgotten that."

" Then how do *you* propose to dodge him ? "

" By altering my appearance." She laughed at his
expression. " You can take it from me, Mr. Smith,
that a girl can alter her appearance very easily. In
fact, we're constantly doing it—and *we* don't need
false moustaches and wigs and whiskers as men do !
Wait a moment ! "

She jumped up and ran into her bedroom. In two
minutes she had reappeared, and he received a shock.
Her hair was plastered down unattractively, she
had done something to her eyes that had taken all the
life and sparkle out of them, and her complexion
was pasty. Giggling, she swung round again,
vanished once more, and returned her original
attractive self. To Simon she seemed more attractive, by comparison with the temporary personality
she had shed. As he stared at her, unable to keep
his bewildered admiration from his eyes, she suddenly became self-conscious, and drew her dressing-
gown a little more closely around her.

" Well ? " she smiled.

" You certainly looked—different," he admitted.

" And yet I was the same person."

" Yes. How on earth did you do it ? "

She laughed. " It was quite easy. So, if that's

settled, we'll work it like this. If there's no policeman at the hotel I return to you and report all clear,
and if there is a policeman—if there *is* a policeman—
then what ? I know. I'll see if I can discover Guest
No. 5 when he turns up, and bring him along, and
you can have your interview in the car instead of in
the hotel. Does that make sense, or not ? "

" Well, it might," he returned, " if you can answer
a couple of questions."

" What are they ? "

" The first is, how are you *going* to discover
Guest No. 5 ? "

" I've a notion, my dear man, that that will be
exceedingly simple. There will be something
fishy about him, and I shall be on the look-out for
what I may describe as internal agitation. Yes, I
believe he'll be easier to smell out than a bad
haddock ! And then, even if I'm not clever enough
to spot him before he makes his inquiry, the inquiry
itself will give him away. He'll ask for Mr. Grainger,
won't he ? Well, then ! So what's the second
question ? "

" Wait a bit ! " exclaimed Simon. " I haven't
quite finished with the first. Yes, he'll ask for Mr.
Grainger, and the policeman may be just as smart on
that as you ! "

" Good point ! " she nodded. " Then I mustn't
let the policeman, if any, be as smart as me ! I must
do my level best to spot the winner—I mean, the
loser—before he gives himself away. Don't worry.
I'll do it. Anyhow, *you've* got to keep out of the
way till we know what's what. Trust Gwendoline
Popchase ! "

" Eh ? "

" My name for my other self. She may be plain,
but she's got a brain ! Next ? "

" The next question," said Simon, " is this.
After you've recognised Guest No. 5, what story
are you going to tell him ? "

" Yes, of course he won't be expecting to meet
Gwen," she responded. " But I've thought of that.
You will arm me with one of your samples, and I'll
dangle a tube of Nugum, casual-like, under his
nose. He will follow it like a donkey after a carrot.
And when we are in a nice, dark corner, I will
whisper, ' Are you wanting to see a man whose
name begins with G ? ' And he will answer, ' Yes,'
' Yus,' or ' Sure, Big Girl,' according to his role.
I'll bet some of these guests are disguised, too ! And
then I'll say, ' Supply the other letters.' And he'll
say, ' R-a-i-n-g-e-r.' And I'll say, ' Right. Follow
me out in a minute, and I'll lead you to him. You
can't meet *here*, for this hotel is under observation.' "

" I've just thought of a third question," Simon
answered, doubt still in his tone.

" Good ! It's better to have them now than later !
What's this one ? "

" You may be able to identify Guest No. 5, but
are you sure you'll be able to identify the policeman ? He'll probably be in plain clothes—like the
one at Bulchester station."

" I'll know him," she said confidently. " You may
not be able to tell a sweep when he's clean, but you
can always tell a policeman whatever he's wearing.
But, of course, if I'm in any doubt, or get in a jam,
I'll return to you without taking action, and we'll
talk it over."

" So long as you promise that, Miss Brown," he

replied, " we'll try your plan, provided we don't think of a better one before the time comes."

There was a pause. They had come to the end of their discussion, and she suddenly held out her hand.

" Good-night, Mr. Smith," she said. " Pleasant dreams."

He took her hand, and made a special point of letting it go before he wanted to.

CHAPTER TWENTY-ONE

AT THE THREE BALLS

NEXT DAY, to Mrs. Mayton's pleasure and surprise, her guests remained with her for breakfast, luncheon, and tea. Again she asked no difficult questions, accepting, without necessarily believing, a rather vague story about some relatives who had to be met at an unnamed station that evening. She was not informed of the alleged situation direct; she gleaned it in scraps of conversation while laying or clearing the table. In the same way she gleaned that her guests were cousins, that through a misunderstanding they had motored up from London a day too soon, and that they were killing time at Five Mile Cottage because it was such a pleasant spot. If it occurred to her as odd that the pleasantness of the spot prevented them from leaving it for even an instant—she had hinted that there were some very pretty walks in the neighbourhood, one to a ruined church well worth visiting—she did not comment on the fact. She enjoyed having young people about the place, and her one real disappointment throughout the day was that she never came upon her guests canoodling.

During the afternoon the sun went in, and after tea the gathering clouds sent down a drizzle. It was still drizzling, and the road was glistening in the dusk, when Milly brought the car out of the shed and they started on their fifty-mile journey to Dill. It had been a queer day. The ordeal at the end of it had loomed gloomily closer as the hours went by, and the breaking of the weather had added to the gloom, but there had been many moments of incongruous pleasure, and in retrospect Simon always remembered the day as a mixture of delight and dread, each holding the other in check. But for the dread, the delight would have been intoxicating ; but for the delight, the dread would have been intolerable. Firm as Simon's intention was to see the matter through, to clear himself and Milly, and to bring retribution down on the heads that deserved it, he had not suddenly developed heroic qualities, and he felt as though he were drawing nearer and nearer to a particularly unpleasant dental appointment.

" I'm not sure that we're going to do fifty miles an hour along these slippery lanes," said Milly.

" Don't try," he suggested.

" I won't," she smiled. " Better to arrive late than never ! "

Nevertheless, her pace seemed quite fast enough to Simon as they slipped along through the fading light, and the falling rain gleamed in the illumination of their head-lamps like moist threads. They spoke little on the journey. On important matters they had said all there was to say, and they were not in a mood for trivialities. Nor did any incident break the half-pleasant, half-uneasy monotony of the drive. But a few miles before it ended, Milly reduced speed and brought the car to a temporary halt.

" What's the matter ? " he asked anxiously.

" Say good-bye to Milly Brown," she replied. " She is about to be replaced by Gwendoline Popchase ! "

The transformation from charm to unattractive-

ness was quickly and deftly effected, and when the
car began to move again, Simon felt as though he
were sitting beside a stranger.

" Well, which do you prefer ? " she inquired, with
a sidelong glance at him.

" Milly Brown," he answered. " You look awful ! "

They reached Dill. In the darkness of a rainy
night, the small town offered no joy to the stranger
and had little to recommend it. It needed, for a
revelation of its few virtues, the assistance of morning sunlight. Suddenly Milly murmured, " Look ! "
Three balls—not pawnbrokers' gold but dull green
—protruded from a building. A large figure stood
in the shadow of a wall, and turned towards them
as they went by. For Milly did not stop. She
continued slowly round the block, bringing the car
to a standstill at the back.

" Now, then ! " she said, sticking out her chin
rather as though she needed to. ". For it ! "

The plan of action had been discussed and agreed,
and then rediscussed and reagreed, but at the
crucial moment Simon hesitated, and she found
his fingers on her arm—the first time he had even
instinctively allowed himself that familiarity.

" What ? " she queried, smiling, as no words came.

" I say ! Be careful ! " he gulped.

" Of course, Simon," she answered. " For both
our sakes."

He stared at her, and then at his fingers, still on
her arm. It seemed to him that, in this moment,
some new world had opened to him to ease the
moment's strain. And yet a girl had merely called
him by his Christian name, in an age when even
" My darling" means nothing, . . . But, after all,

did it ease the strain ? Was the strain not abruptly, violently increased ?

"Look here ! You—you *mustn't* get into any trouble," he faltered. " I mean—that would be awful ! "

" I won't," she replied, "if you'll make me the same promise."

" I can't possibly get into any trouble waiting here," he returned.

She recalled the unjustified confidence later, although at the moment she shared it. Otherwise she would not have opened the door of the car and stepped out on to the dark, wet pavement.

" Well, see you don't," she said through the window, " and I'll see I don't."

He called after her, just before she vanished :

" Whoa ! Wait ! How long do I give you, if you don't come back ? "

" If nothing happens in, say, half an hour, you might come round very, very cautiously," she suggested. " But don't forget that I may have to be away for some while." Then she disappeared, the glistening mist of rain almost blotting her out before she was round the corner.

He lit a cigarette, and then turned his head to regard the empty driver's seat. He longed for it to be occupied again. Simon ! It had always seemed an absurd name to him. He had never realised that the word could sound so good . . . !

Milly had to turn two corners. After rounding the first she hurried, in obedience to a primitive instinct against getting wet, but before she reached the second she slackened speed, adopting a casual manner that, in the circumstances, was a little too

casual. She realised this suddenly as she came in
sight of the Three Balls, the three globular green
symbols of which dripped over the door on to the
pavement.

" I am trying to be natural," she told herself
admonishingly, " and here I am walking through
rain as though it were sunshine."

But she was grateful to her error, for it was the con-
sciousness of it that gave her the next brainwave.

" I've got to have some reason for entering the
hotel," she thought. " What better than the
weather ? "

So now, again slightly overdoing it, she stared
upwards, got a mouthful, exclaimed loudly, " Goodness ! This rain ! " and dashed into the hotel, nearly
knocking an old man over as she did so.

" Oh dear ! I'm so sorry ! " she gushed.   " I've
just rushed in from the rain ! "

In response to this superfluous information, the
old man stepped aside, murmuring politely, " That's
all right. No damage." Then he added, " Yes, it is
terrible weather, terrible. I just came to have a look
at it myself."

He returned to a well-worn arm-chair under a
clock which he had vacated for his meteorological
survey, took up an evening paper, and vanished
behind it. The clock above him said twenty-six
minutes past eight.

The hotel lobby was little more than a rather
wide and long passage, with open doors on either
side and a staircase towards the end. A smell of
cooking pervaded the smoky atmosphere, like a bad
advertisement for eating. A stout man came out of
one of the rooms, and looked at Milly inquiringly.

"I've come in to be out of the rain," explained Milly. "Is that all right?"

"Yes, certainly, miss," replied the man, with a vague loss of interest. She did not, after all, represent profit.

He turned round and went into the room again. The old man under the clock remained buried in his newspaper. A woman came out of another room, complaining to anybody who liked to hear about the poor quality of the coffee. She complained all the way up the flight of stairs at the back, her voice continuing even when only her feet were visible. A depressed waiter appeared from the room. "Life is like this," said his expression. "There is nothing one can do about it." The old man, without unsheathing his face from his newspaper, asked him the time as he passed. The waiter looked up at the clock above him and said, "Half-past eight, sir," and the clock corroborated his statement by striking the half-hour wheezily.

The waiter paused before Milly.

"No. 6?" he inquired.

The voice of the stout man sounded:

"No, no, that's not No. 6. The lady's waiting till the rain stops."

If the rain stopped, would she have to go? Perhaps she had better order a cup of coffee. . . .

"I'm sorry, madam," murmured the depressed waiter, "but someone was asking just now if No. 6 had arrived yet."

Milly's heart missed a beat. "The gentleman sitting in that chair?" she replied casually.

"Er—yes, miss."

"Poor man! If there's one thing I hate myself,

R.N.S.   O

it's waiting for people, especially when they don't turn up. Could I have a cup of coffee? "

" Certainly. The coffee-room is on your right."

" Thank you, but I'd rather have it out here, if you don't mind. At that little table."

The little table was beside the arm-chair in which the old man was sitting. On the other side was a stiff wooden chair. She took it as the waiter departed. The complaining woman came down the stairs again, still complaining. " *What* is the use of ringing a bell? " she demanded.

As she disappeared to repeat the question to the stout manager, Milly addressed the unseen face behind the newspaper on the opposite side of the little table. She did not notice that the newspaper had a small hole in it, to which the old man's eye was glued.

" Some people have no patience at all," she remarked.

" Eh? " exclaimed the old man, now lowering the paper.

" You have some, anyway," continued Milly, conversationally.

" And what makes you think that? " inquired the old man.

" Well, didn't I understand just now that you are waiting for somebody? "

" Maybe, young lady, you are, also? "

The old man's eyes smiled, but she knew he was studying her closely.

" What I'm waiting for," she answered, " is a cup of coffee."

" Ah, coffee," murmured the old man. " I see. Just coffee. Now, I had an idea—of course, I may be quite wrong, in which case you will forgive me—I had an idea that you might be waiting for a gentleman of the name of Grainger ? "

" What makes *you* think that ? " asked Milly.

His question did not quite fit.

The old man continued to smile. The waiter brought the coffee. Then the old man bent forward and observed:

" Perhaps the wish was father to the thought. It would have interested me."

" Why ? "

" Because, young lady, I *am* Mr. Grainger."

It was a difficult moment. The table swayed a little, and the coffee she was raising to her lips nearly missed her mouth. . . . Was there, then, a *real* Mr. Grainger ?

" You look surprised," commented the old man.

" Only because I—I thought you were asking for Mr. Grainger," she answered.

" Really ? But what made you think that ? " he blinked innocently. " I overheard your conversation with the waiter. He said that I had inquired for, as he put it, ' No. 6.' Suppose—just for the sake of argument—an academic point—suppose I had ? There was no mention of the name of Grainger."

" But you mentioned the name," retorted Milly, her mind spinning.

" Most certainly," agreed the old man.

" And so I just put two and two together."

" Or, should you have said, six and six ? " The old man shook his head, with tolerant reproof. " I think, perhaps, we have reached a point in our acquaintance when we can dispense with both names and numbers. You, quite obviously, are not

Mr. Grainger. And since you now know my own
identity, perhaps I may learn a little more about
yours. What, young lady, can I do for you ? "

The question was too vital for an immediate
answer. Half her coffee remained in the cup. She
drank it with deliberate slowness, without tasting it.
If it had been the vilest coffee ever made, and it
nearly was, she would not have known it. Afterwards, when the cup was empty, she counted ten in
her mind. Then she said:

" Isn't the next step some proof of identity ? "

" You are a very cautious young lady," replied
the old man.

" You should be the first to realise that necessity."

" True. But—whose identity ? "

" Yours, of course."

" Why not yours ? "

" I haven't stated mine yet."

" True again. Kindly state it."

" That would put the cart before the horse."

The old man smiled, with a sort of despairing
admiration.

" Young lady," he said, " and I continue to call
·you young lady because so far you refuse to provide
me with any substitute—young lady, one day when
we have more time you shall tell me where you
studied the art of evasive conversation. But, unfortunately, we have not much time, as a clock ticking
above my head proclaims. Before I give you my
proof of identity, let me know why you require it.
Do you doubt that I am Mr. Grainger—of Room
No. 6 ? "

" I haven't said so," she retorted quickly.

" No, merely implied it."

" Or used just natural caution."

" I admit the theory, but prefer to develop my own. If you doubt that I am Mr. Grainger, that must be because you already know Mr. Grainger in some other guise. Well ? Do you ? "

" What ? " she stammered.

" And, if you do, I should be interested to meet him."

Milly felt herself flushing. She was furious with herself, but the situation was beating her. She could understand Guest No. 5 hesitating to reveal himself to a stranger, but why should he declare himself to be the person he had come to meet ? Was the old man Guest No. 5 ? Might he not, after all, be some original Mr. Grainger for whom Simon was unconsciously passing himself ? Whoever the old man was, who did he assume *her* to be . . . ?

All at once she found the old man looking at her with a new intentness. Because she could not think of anything else to do, and because she did not want to display any psychological inferiority, she replied in kind. For several seconds they maintained this rude scrutiny, while the complaining woman emerged from the manager's room exclaiming, " Well, there it is ! If I don't get service, I go ! " They heard her indignant footsteps mounting the overworked stairs. Then the old man said :

" Tell me ! *Have* you a more attractive method of doing your hair ? "

Milly's mouth opened. And, as her vis-a-vis smiled at her, she counter-attacked.

" And what's the betting," she retorted, " that *your* hair is a wig ? "

" It is a wig, young lady," answered the old man.

" Inspector Davis, at your service. And now, please, take me to see Mr. Grainger."

Milly's mind moved swiftly and accurately through her confusion. The police had turned up again, and this was not the moment for another flight. And she liked the inspector's smile.

" My name is Milly Brown," she said. " I think you want to see me as much as Mr. Grainger. Returning frankness for frankness, I'm the person who drove from Bulchester to London and who passed herself off as a journalist at Mr. Mildenhall's flat."

" That is interesting."

" And so is this. Someone is coming here to-night to meet Mr. Grainger—I thought at first that you were the person, and perhaps you thought I was ! —and if you don't interfere with our plan, we may collect a big bag for you. So now what ? "

Davis glanced quickly round the hall. No one occupied it saving themselves. The clock above the table wheezed the quarter-to. When Davis spoke, his voice was quiet and businesslike.

" Where's Grainger now ? " he asked.

" In our car, at the back of the block," answered Milly.

" Why ? "

" I came round first to see whether the coast was clear."

" And it wasn't ? "

" No. We didn't want you around till afterwards."

" Again, why ? "

" Is there time to explain ? Perhaps we felt we'd been foolish, and wanted to whitewash ourselves. Perhaps we were really pretty—pretty livid over the murder of our Chief—Mildenhall—and perhaps we were afraid that a policeman might scare our visitor off——"

" In other words, you didn't trust the police," interposed the inspector.

" Call us idiots," murmured Milly, refusing to exonerate herself from a share in the blame.

" With pleasure," answered the inspector, " since I have already formed the opinion that you are nothing worse. This visitor you mention doesn't seem to have arrived here yet."

" No."

" Then how about nipping round to the car, sending Mr. Grainger here, and assuring him that an old gentleman with white hair sitting under a clock will do nothing to interfere with his plan ? Incidentally, Miss Brown, if the plan goes wrong, and if Mr. Smith, alias Grainger, finds himself in any difficulty with a dangerous crook, it may be just as well to have a policeman on the premises. Don't you think ? "

" It seems to me," she said, " that after all our mistrust of him, the policeman is being rather a brick."

It was still raining as she left the hotel. She ran round the block, but stopped short when she had rounded the second corner. She was facing the rear of the car, and had a vague, smudgy view of the driver's seat. It was occupied. Not by Simon, but by a bulky form. She saw it dimly through the moist glass.

As she stood and stared, the car began to move. With a gasp she ran forward again, but she was too late. The car slid away and vanished into the murk.

CHAPTER TWENTY-TWO

THE FIFTH

Two MINUTES after Milly's departure from the car, Simon turned his head. Someone was approaching, and he thought at first that it was Milly returning. Instead, a large Negro materialised outside the window-glass, and opened the door as though it were his.

" Massa Grainger ? " he inquired.

The question was asked with complete assurance, and if the idea of prevarication had entered Simon's head, instinct would have dismissed it as useless. But the idea did not enter his head. Dismayed though he was by the nature of his visitor, he identified him as the expected No. 5, and secretly congratulated his working partner on the speed with which she had played her part. A policeman, he assumed, *had* been discovered in the hotel, and Milly had tipped Guest No. 5 the wink. Only in the first half of this surmise was he correct.

" Yes, I am Mr. Grainger," he answered. " I suppose the hotel was—er—not quite healthy for our chat ? "

The Negro grinned as he stepped into the car and took the driving seat, closing the door after him.

" Tha's so ! " he nodded. " I guess hotel no good, so I stayed outside. In heah it is better ! "

The Negro's bulk was an unpleasant exchange for Milly's neat figure, seeming like a sacrilegious invasion of hallowed space, but it had to be borne. It was all part and parcel, came the comforting reflection, of their joint plan, and the fact that Milly had done her part so well and expeditiously stiffened Simon in his determination to make no failure of his.

" Let's get our credentials over quickly," he said, in the voice he had used when he had been miscast as a crook on his one and only appearance in amateur theatricals. " We've got a lot to talk about. You're satisfied, I suppose, with mine ? "

" Sure ! You are Massa Grainger," nodded the Negro.

" So who are you ? " asked Simon. " You know, of course, that I have to go through the formality of establishing your name ? "

" Establishing your name " was good ! For the first time in this taxing adventure, Simon felt a little pleased with himself. If only he could keep this up . . .

" Sure, I know that," the Negro interrupted his thoughts. " Sure, I know a mouthful ! My name is Mr. Micklemoses."

" Try again," suggested Simon.

The Negro's grin expanded.

" Smart fellah ! " he commented.

" We need to be, you and me," answered Simon.

" Sure ! " The Negro closed his eyes, and opened them. The whites of his eyes made two unpleasant rims in the darkness of the car. " You got something for me, Massa Grainger ? "

" I'm still waiting for something from you," retorted Simon. " That name."

" O.K. Sam Monday. You like that bettah ? "

" Much better." Monday had six letters in it, which was why he had disbelieved Micklemoses. " Now we know each other, Mr. Monday."

" Tha's so ! "

He extended a dark paw in Simon's direction. With considerable distaste, Simon shook it. The Negro frowned, then smiled.

" You think I ask for yo' hand ? " he inquired. " Oh, no, Massa Grainger. I ask for something else."

" You'll get that," replied Simon.

" Sure, I will ! "

" But first let's talk about things."

" What things ? "

" Things we've all got to talk about. I suppose you know—all the others ? "

" Others ? "

" Come, come, Mr. Monday ! Do you think I'm quite the fool I look ? "

" Sure, I hope not ! " exclaimed Mr. Samuel Monday, but he seemed a little impressed.

" Then I don't need to tell you who these others are ! You know them ? "

Simon continued to marvel at himself. He was acting as hard as he had acted in that amateur show, and, it seemed, with better success. This was strange, for he was even more nervous, a condition which, at the original performance, had seemed impossible.

" I know some," murmured the Negro.

" Not all ? "

" Mebbe."

" And you've seen them lately ? Since Monday ? You're in touch with them ? "

Suspicion entered the Negro's eyes.

"What make you ask that, Massa Grainger?"
he queried.

"I'll tell you," answered Simon. "It's because
I'm not satisfied with the way things are going.
Are *you*?"

The Negro frowned.

"What yo' mean by that?" he demanded.
"Sure, I'm not satisfied if you don' gimme what I'm
heah for!"

"Oh, you'll get that," said Simon, "just as the
others did. D'you suppose I'm a double-crosser?"
He perspired as he used the term, and wished he
hadn't. He went on quickly, "But, well, murders
don't help us, do they? And we've had a couple
already!"

He felt the Negro's eyes burning into him with
curiosity.

"No, murders don' help us," he agreed solemnly.
"But I don' murder, sure!" He added, with the
grin that was never far off, "Not yet, I don'!"

"But you know some who *do* murder," said
Simon. "You know the—the weak links in our
chain, just as well as I do."

Again the grin vanished, and solemnity returned.

"Sure! I know!"

"And are you quite happy about it?"

"Go on."

"It's your turn. I've asked you a question."

"So yo' did."

"Well?"

"What's in yo' mind?"

"All right, I'll tell you," said Simon. "*I'm* not
happy about it. The—the damn' police are getting
too close. But, well, the damage is done, and we

can't go back on it, so what we've got to do is to
get together and—and thrash the matter out. If we
don't, we'll all be in the soup—those who haven't
done these murders as well as those who have ! Do
you get the idea ? "

The Negro looked thoughtful, then shook his head.

" I'm still waitin' to heah yo' idea," he said.

" I may not be the only one with an idea,"
answered Simon, deciding that a little modesty
might be wise, " but I've got one, and if things work
out right, I dare say you'll all agree it's a good one
when I tell it to you."

" Oh ! And when yo' tell it to us ? "

" To-morrow."

" Where ? "

" The Black Swan, Enford."

Now a faint smile entered the Negro's face. He
evidently knew the address.

" And who will be at the Black Swan, Enford ? "
he inquired, blinking.

" I will, and you will, and all the others, if you
bring them along. Listen, Mr. Monday," Simon
continued, as he saw hesitation in the Negro's eyes.
" I know what I'm talking about, and one thing I
know is that to clear out of this mess we'll need
money. Yes, more than there is in that envelope
you're waiting for ! Some of us may have to leave
the country for a long while, and you can't do that
without a bit in your pocket. And I happen to know
where to get that bit."

" Where ? "

" Would you mention it, in my place ? After all,
Mr. Monday, you and I have only just met, you
know."

" Sure ! "

" There's safety in numbers, and I hope there'll be a good number at the Black Swan to-morrow night at —let's say—nine o'clock. Then you shall hear everything. Meanwhile, don't forget, although I didn't kill Mr. Mildenhall any more than you did, I was with him last Monday at his London flat, and perhaps I didn't waste my time there. Well, what about it ? Is it O.K. with you ? "

Something sounded on the pavement behind them. The Negro turned his head.

" Sure, it's O.K. with me," he murmured.

The blow on Simon's chin was so swift and so accurate that he did not even know the car had started to move.

CHAPTER TWENTY-THREE

THE LAST ON THE LIST

SIMON opened his eyes, then quickly closed them again. He was not in a car ; he was half under a table in a smoke-sodden room, bound hand and foot. He closed his eyes for three reasons, any one of which would have been sufficient alone. The first was that he felt dizzy. His jaw ached, his head ached, his whole body ached. The second was that he preferred darkness, even darkness with vague lights darting about, to the view he had opened his eyes to. And the third was because two men who composed a part of the view—they were seated at the other end of the room, and he could glimpse a portion of their backs—were apparently not aware that their victim's senses were returning, and it occurred to the victim that it would be a good idea to keep this knowledge from them for as long as possible. One of the men was a hairy-armed fellow in his shirt-sleeves. The other was Mr. Samuel Monday, the Negro.

"And so that's what happened, is it ? " exclaimed the hairy-armed one.

"Sure, tha's what happened," answered the Negro. " So I brought him along."

"What made you suspect him ? "

"Oh, I done suspect him from the start," drawled the Negro boastfully. " I can smell a rat as well as nobody ! "

" Of course, you'd been warned by the bunch ? "

" I didn't need no warnin'. All niggers ain't got thick skulls. I'm smart."

" Of course you are, Mr. Monday ! "

" Of course I am, Massa Kurd. Monday ! " He laughed. " And what was *yo'* new name goin' to be ? "

There was a short pause. Then the red-haired man answered :

" That don't matter now, for the fellow under the table won't need to hear it—nor anybody else, eh ? And besides, Sam, if you're as smart as you say, I expect you brought along more than our fool, Mr. Grainger ? I expect you brought along a couple of sealed envelopes instead of one. And you ain't forgetting, are you, that the t'other one belongs to me ? Come on ! Let's have it ! "

" For nothin', Massa Kurd ? "

" Look sharp ! I can be smart, too ! "

There was another short pause, during which Simon gathered that the last of the six envelopes was handed over.

" O.K., Massa Kurd," said the Negro. " Sure, you're smart, too. And our fool friend heah was some smart, sure he was, I'll say, when I said my name was somethin'-else-or-other. He counted up the letters and found there was too many."

" Oh, did he ? " exclaimed Kurd, clearly interested. " Was he on to it ? "

" On to what ? "

Kurd laughed. " I'd forgotten. I'm the only one, eh, the Boss tells all his little secrets to ? The rest of you just give your new names, like good little children, and take your pay, and know nothing ! "

" Mebbe we'd like to know more, Massa Kurd."

" Speaking just for yourself ? "

" Mebbe—not ! "

" Oho ! So you've all been meeting ? "

" Mebbe yeah ! "

" I see. Breaking the Boss's orders——"

" Things is gettin' hot, Massa Kurd," interrupted the Negro. " Yeah, we had a meetin'. Massa Grainger, he no good to us no more, and police all over the shop ! We gotta get out and clear out. We gotta see this heah Boss ! He done hide himself enough, sure ! We gotta have more money."

Kurd did not reply. Simon heard his steps crossing the floor towards him. He did his best to appear limp, and had no difficulty. The steps reached him and stopped, and then followed breathing as Kurd's body stooped.

" Some Joe Louis blow, what ? " came the Negro's voice, in a vain purr.

" If he's dead," answered Kurd, " who's going to swing for him ? "

" Not me ! "

With relief, Simon heard the steps retreating.

" And who's going to swing for Mildenhall and that policeman ? " continued Kurd scornfully. " A nice team I picked for the Boss ! No. 1 gets greedy, and kills the golden goose ! No. 2—she was going to meet No. 1 and share the swag with him—on terms. She made the terms, but she'd never have kept 'em with that ex-bruiser ! No. 3, trying to succeed where No. 1 failed, falls foul of a copper, and bumps *him* off ! He ought to have kept inside the hotel, like he began, instead of getting himself shut out ! No. 4

pounced on his pound of flesh like a frightened rabbit ! And No. 5———"

" Tha's me," the Negro reminded him. " I'm smart, if the rest ain't ! "

" Maybe you are—maybe you're not. The game's not over yet, you know ! "

" Sure it ain't. You're No. 6."

" I'm No. 6———"

" Who knows a mouthful about the other five ! "

" Does that surprise you ? I'm the Boss's right-hand man, aren't I ? The Boss don't hide nothing from me, and I keep my eyes open for the Boss. . . . And so you all want to meet the Boss, eh ? "

" That so."

" And what's the big idea, when you've met him ? "

" We gotta talk about things."

" What things ? "

" He take the big money, we take the big risk———"

" Oh, yes, I remember. You're after more dough. But what's *he* going to say about it ? "

" If he talk plenty, we talk plenty," retorted the Negro doggedly. " We gotta finish up this and get out of it."

" I see," answered Kurd. " Sounds rather like a frame-up to me."

Now came a long silence. Simon interpreted it as a calm before a storm. It was ended, however, by Kurd's soft laughter.

" Maybe you're right," he said. " Maybe it's a good idea. Maybe—I'll help you. But you know, of course, that no one has ever got the better of the Boss yet ? "

" No ? " queried the Negro.

There was a touch of scepticism in his tone.

" Who ? " demanded Kurd.

" I heah some rumour that Massa Mildenhall did,"
answered the Negro.

" Well, that's true—but it was only at first,"
replied Kurd slowly, " and the Boss don't care who
laughs so long as he laughs last. As he always does !
How much do you know ? "

The Negro considered his response, then gave it
in the drawl that eggs a man on.

" I know that Mildenhall fooled him, sure ! "

" Who told you ? "

" These things get about."

" Then you'd better hear the correct version—to
correct any false ideas you're getting about the
Boss ! Listen ! "

" I listen best with a glass in my hand."

Drinks were poured out. The sound of the liquid
was tantalising to the bound man on the floor. His
throat was parched.

" Do you know this, to begin with ? " asked
Kurd, after a draught. " Do you know why the
Boss first went to Mildenhall's flat ? "

" I guess it wasn't to play dominoes, and I guess
it wasn't through the front door."

" Right both times ! It was for the Mildenhall
formula, and it was through a window. The formula
—you know this ?—was an inoculation against gas,
and the Boss had got wind of it and mentioned it to
a certain foreign Government. The foreign Govern-
men offered a big price. . . . Of course, the Boss
didn't know that anybody was at home when he
called at the flat the first time, but unfortunately
Mildenhall was at home with a revolver. Oh, yes !

The Boss lost the first round. He admits that all
right. He was bound up as tightly as that fellow
under the table there, and after that he was the
victim of the dirtiest trick that was ever played.
Stuck in a room for six days, he was, and used for
experimental purposes. Like a rabbit in a laboratory ! "

" My, my ! " murmured the Negro.

Kurd spat, then continued :

" The formula wasn't quite complete, Mildenhall
told him, and a test was needed on a human being.
The Boss was that human being. The snag was that
the cure might kill, and it would take six days to
find out. The Boss's arm was punctured, and the
test began."

" Massa Mildenhall, he must have been some
mad," observed the Negro.

" He was," replied Kurd. " But the Boss was
some madder when, after going through six days of
hell, he was set free and informed that he had
merely been punctured, and not inoculated at all !
He'd sweated for nothing. ' That'll teach you,'
jeered Mildenhall, as he kicked him out of the door.
Kicked him out ! The Boss ! "

" I guess Mildenhall made a mistake there,"
commented the Negro.

" By God, he did ! " exclaimed Kurd. " The Boss
swore to get even with him, and that the number 6
should be branded on his brain. He waited for
his chance, which came on Thursday of last week,
and called again. This time Mildenhall *was* out—
and Mildenhall's daughter was in. And when
Mildenhall returned to his flat, he found not only
the formula gone, but also his daughter. And,

incidentally, several tubes of a new gum he was going to put on the market. And that evening he received a phone from the Boss, and was told just what to do."

" To get his daughter back ? "

" Of course ! Now, listen. Mildenhall had called the Boss a fool. Lacking in brain and ingenuity. A coward. Every name under the sun during those six days of hell. Well, the Boss didn't much care for that, you know—he's always been rather proud of his brain and his ingenuity. And, if there's a debt, he always pays in kind. So he concocted this scheme by which Mildenhall should suffer six days of torture, while his daughter went through what the Boss had gone through. The girl, inoculated with his stuff, was stowed away at an address which Mildenhall would learn, bit by bit, paying through the nose for the knowledge. Not till the sixth day after the inoculation—that's to-morrow—would he have the address complete. Then he could go and collect the girl, either dead or alive, as the case might be ! No brains, eh ? Every detail was worked out ! No ingenuity, eh ? The team was collected——"

" Through you ? "

" You know that ! Through me. I always know where to pick 'em up ! But that darned fool under the table was picked by Mildenhall, out of the applicants for a job the Boss advertised. I reckon Mildenhall gave up thinking the Boss had no ingenuity before he died ! "

He paused.

The Negro asked :

" Why didn't Mildenhall go to the police ? "

" For the reason," answered Kurd obviously,

" that the Boss had told him over the phone what would happen to his daughter if he did. See ? "

" Yeah ! But I don't see why Mildenhall left London and went to Brackham."

" We'll never know that. He's beyond telling us ! P'raps he got the wind up. P'raps he lost his head. P'raps he wanted to keep an eye on his new employee, or give some new instruction, or take on the job himself. Yes, what about that ? Maybe he decided he'd be Room No.6 himself, eh, and that's why he rigged himself up with his false moustache and so on ? And, passing off at first as the first visitor, wanted to test whether the chap he'd engaged recognised him ? That would have been smart, I'll admit. Only the trouble with Mildenhall's smartness was that it didn't last the course ! Anyway, all that don't matter now. He's dead. And the Boss is alive."

" And the girl ? " inquired the Negro.

" The girl ? Well, that's what the Boss will find out to-morrow when he goes to see her. And that's what Mildenhall would have found out to-morrow if things had gone to plan and he'd lived to learn the address."

" And that's where *we* want to go to-morrow."

" If you're still dead nuts on seeing the Boss ? "

" We sure are."

" How much do you mean to stick him for ? "

" As much as he'll fork out. We want to do some laughing, too."

" I've told you, you remember, that he's a sleuth on that last laugh ? "

" Sure, you've told me."

" Suppose he turns the tables on you ? "

" He won't do that."

" Very well. I'm not saying you're wrong, I'm only warning you. And now I've done that, maybe I'll come along, too, and join in the fun ! Now, then ! See here ! Those six names the Boss invented for you——" ,

" We know only five," interposed the Negro.

" Yes, but mine was the sixth. Not Kurd, of course. *Nor* Sweden. Here ! Let's write 'em all down. Where's a bit of paper ? . . . Now, here we go."

There was a short silence. Simon heard the sound of a pencil-stump being used heavily. He risked opening his eyes, and saw the backs of the two men, bending over what Kurd had written.

" There we are," said Kurd. " There's your five names, and here's mine added. Not Sweden, but next door to it. Neat, eh ? The Boss sent him a post card asking, ' What's in a name ? ' Some jest, eh ? "

" That don't tell me nothin'," murmured the Negro.

" It will, when I mention one other point," replied Kurd. " You remember the Boss was punctured on the arm ? "

" Sure, I remember."

" Well, he was punctured quite a number of times, and in the form of a cross. The Boss reminded Mildenhall of this when he phoned him up last week."

There was another silence. A shorter one, broken by the Negro's whistle. " So, that's it," he exclaimed.

" That's it," answered Kurd. " And now we'll burn it, eh ? "

He rose from his chair, and Simon quickly closed his eyes again. He heard the striking of a match.

" Is that enough address ? " asked the Negro.

" Quite enough," replied Kurd. " It's a small village, and the postmistress, who sells sweets as well as stamps, will direct any one. But she don't send no letters there, because it's been empty for donkey's years—ever since the Boss took it for his own private purposes. . . . Well, Mr. Samuel Monday, all I've got to do now is to add the time of to-morrow's appointment—9 p.m.—and all *you've* got to do is to get in touch again with the rest of the bunch and pass the good news on. So there we are ! "

" Sure, there we are," answered the Negro.

And now he rose, too, and extended his hand. Simon saw the final handshake through half-closed lids. The faces of the two men were presented to him in profile. The Negro's black and grinning ; Kurd's cynical, but also smiling. Simon noticed something else as well, though it made no special impression on him at the moment. It recurred to him afterwards. One of Kurd's shirtsleeves had come unfastened and was hanging loose.

A moment later the Negro had vanished, and the door had closed behind him.

Kurd turned. Simon's eyes closed completely as he did so. After a short interval, during which no sound broke an unearthly stillness, Kurd laughed.

" I'll deal with you under the table there in a minute," he said, " but there's another little bunch I've got to fix up first ! Want to meet the Boss, do they ? Well, they'll meet somebody, only it won't be the Boss ! " His voice imitated his late visitor. " Sure ! "

He crossed to a wall. Simon heard the tinkle of a phone. Then he heard something else, unheard by Kurd himself. A door softly opening.

Kurd's voice came :

" Hallo ! Hallo ! Give me the police station——"

Then another :

" Put that down, Boss ! I saw those marks on yo' arm ! Sure ! "

Kurd dropped the receiver in its place and swung round with an oath.

" What the hell ! " he shouted.

" You Goddam double-crosser ! " replied the Negro.

Kurd's bullet missed. The Negro's knife, passing like lightning through three yards of space, found its mark. Kurd fell, and did not rise. His head struck the floor within an inch of Simon's feet.

" Well, Massa Kurd," sounded the Negro's smooth voice. " Who laughs last ? "

CHAPTER TWENTY-FOUR

SOLUTION OF A PUZZLE

EXACTLY what happened after that Simon did not know. Whether he gave himself away and brought the menace of the Negro to his side, or whether the Negro already knew that his victim was not dead, remained a matter of debate. But additional pains when he next emerged from the blackness into which he suddenly relapsed suggested that he had received some further very rough treatment ; and, but for sudden new arrivals who hastened the Negro's departure, that unpleasant individual might have completed a second murder with the object of escaping suspicion for the first. That was the theory of Inspector Davis, who had had some experience of the wiles of the crooked. Dead men tell no tales.

But it was not to the inspector that Simon opened his eyes many hours later. Milly Brown was seated beside the bed in which he found himself, and the sight was so staggeringly wonderful and completely unexpected that he promptly went back into the blackness for a space. Half an hour later he opened his eyes again, to discover that Milly was still there.

" How—what—where—— ? " he mumbled.

" Don't talk," ordered Milly. " We're here, and everything's all right. Go to sleep again."

That seemed the pleasantest thing to do. To go to sleep, with Milly sitting by his side. And to complete the amazing perfection of the moment, her hand reached forward and touched his. But the moment did not last. Horrible memories were invading the maze of his mind. Something had to be done—something—something—and he couldn't think what !

" I told you to go to sleep," repeated Milly. " Stop frowning ! I'll smooth your forehead."

Now he felt her touch on his brow. He tried to get rid of his oppressions. He didn't want anything but just this. But the oppressions persisted, battling against the soothing sensation of cool fingers. . . .

Suddenly he sat up.

" Lie down ! " she admonished.

" The names ! Those names ! " he spluttered.

" Never mind about names—never mind about anything," she ordered.

" We've got to ! My head ! Yes, but I can't help that—we've got to ! Has any one been caught yet ? "

She looked at him concernedly.

" We just missed someone when we got here——"

" Here ? "

" The Black Swan. Don't you know ? When we found you'd gone I nearly went batty——"

" We ? I—I don't quite—is there someone else ? "

" A detective, but don't worry—everything's explained to him, and he's all right. We hunted for you hopelessly till I remembered the name of the final hotel on your list—thank God I knew it !—and we tried that as a last resource. And—well, we found you here, and put you to bed——"

" Was I alone ? "

" Yes. I told you we just missed somebody. I think he got out of a window. We heard his car go off, and nobody else was here . . . no one alive. . . . I wish you'd go to sleep again."

"I can't ! Go on, go on ! " he begged.

"All right. Don't get excited ! We put you to bed, and the detective continued the hunt, and left me here. There's a policeman on duty below, and a doctor has been, and declared that you'll live, so now, *please*——"

"Where's the detective hunting ? "

"Oh dear ! I don't know ! "

"Hasn't he got a clue or anything ? "

"They always have clues, don't they ? I was told to get the policeman up when you could ' make a statement,' as they call it, only—really, *really*, dear —just a short snooze—there's no hurry——"

"Hurry ! My God, isn't there ? " He tried to get out of bed, but she pressed him back. "Those names ! What's the matter with me ? I'm wasting time ! Yes, what time is it ? "

Despairingly she glanced at a clock.

"Twelve past six."

"What ? In the morning ? "

"No, evening."

He stared at her with feverish eyes.

"Twelve past six ! And they said nine. But will they go there now ? They may ! Yes, I expect they will. And even if they don't, there's the girl."

"What girl ? "

She thought he was raving.

"Eh ? Miss Mildenhall."

"*What !* "

"Where's some paper ! Quick ! And a pencil." Confused as he was, he interpreted her intention when she ran to the door. "No, don't get the policemen yet. Please, Milly ! Miss Brown ! Milly ! Don't mind what I say, you see how I am. But I'd

rather work this out here just quietly, with you.
Paper ! Where is it ? " She began running about.
" The six names, you know. And the cross. That'll
give it. And if it doesn't seem enough, the woman
at the post office—remember that, if I forget it.
The woman at the post office. She'll—ah, thank
you ! "

She had found an envelope, and brought it to
him. A moment later she had added a pencil. But
when he seized the pencil he found he could not
write. His fingers were too limp.

" Funny ! Sort of numb," he muttered. " You
write. I'll tell you. The names—one after the
other. Quick ! I'm losing them ! "

She took the envelope and pencil, her heart beating
furiously. Simon looking very queer.

" Take it slowly," she said.

" That's right. Slowly. It's all right if I just go
slowly. Now, then. Raikes. R-a-i-k-e-s. He told
me how to spell it. Well, of course he did ! What ?
Second, Rodent. No, wait ! Searle. S-e-a-r-l-e. Got
that ? "

She nodded. His mind went blank.

" Third, Rodent," she said, bending close to his
ear. " I know them all but the last two. Fourth,
Godwin. Fifth—— ? "

" Monday," he whispered.

" And the last ? "

She waited. His eyes closed. She put her mouth
against his ear.

" And the last ? " she repeated. " The sixth
name ? Do you remember it ? " He made no
response. He was slipping away. " Can you hear
this, then ? I love you, Simon." His eyes came

open through shock. " That last name ? What was it ? "

" Eh ? What ? . . . I . . . Not Sweden. . . ."

That was all he could manage before drifting off into his most bewildering black-out.

She knew it had to be six letters. " Norway," she wrote. She was still poring over the names when Inspector Davis returned for news. He, to his despair, had none.

She told him hers, while Simon slept peacefully.

" He looks better," grunted Davis, and then began studying the six names himself.

" Let's try 'em this way," he said. " Not in a string. One under another."

He wrote them thus :

RAIKES

SEARLE

RODENT

GODWIN

MONDAY

NORWAY

" And now, what about this cross ? " he went on.

" If you mean the cross is going to indicate the letters," answered Milly, " where are you going to draw it ? If you put it symmetrically bang in the centre, it doesn't touch any letters but goes through space."

" The letters over and under the horizontal line being Rodent and Godwin——" began Davis.

" And the letters on either side of the vertical line being Iaddnr and Krewdw," finished Milly. " So that's no good ! "

" Yes, but there's more than one kind of cross,"
said Davis. " We've tried the one that means
addition. Let's try the one that means multiplica-
tion. Corner to corner."

Two seconds later Milly's heart bounded.

" Redway," she spelt, from the north-west corner
to the south-east.

" Sledon," spelt Davis, from the north-east to the
south-west. " Redway, Sledon."

He ran from the room, and was back three minutes
later.

" I've phoned to the station," he exclaimed,
" and there's a Sledon in Essex. They got through
to Sledon while I waited, and Redway's a house
there all right. I'm off at once ! " He glanced at
the peaceful form in the bed. " You'll wait here ? "

" My job's here," she answered. " But what do I
do the next time he wakes up ? "

" Get his story, and phone it through, and I'll
pick it up at the police station at the other end."

She nodded, then reminded him, " You've not
forgotten he mentioned something about nine
o'clock ? "

" I've not forgotten," replied the inspector. " I
shall make it ! "

CHAPTER TWENTY-FIVE

AT a quarter to nine, under a heavy drizzling night sky, the Negro pushed open a creaking gate and passed through, with the softness of a cat, into a dark and overgrown drive. For a man of his bulk he trod the gravel with remarkable lightness. He was rather like a materialised shadow, moving stealthily among other shadows that were stationary ; but some of the other shadows whispered and waved and rustled as he continued on his way past tangled bushes and overhanging trees towards the house at the end of the drive. He paused on that short, curved journey several times. He didn't much care for the whispering and the waving and the rustling, and he wished he had closed the gate behind him instead of letting it swing back and close itself with a sharp little click. Still, his mood was cautious rather than anxious, for he was feeling very pleased with himself, and recent events had developed his superiority complex.

When he reached the house, he stood outside the dilapidated porch for several seconds, staring at the door and the windows. The rain drizzled down into his eyes, and he liked the feel of it. He liked the look of the house, too, as dilapidated as the porch, and as deserted, if one could judge by appearances, as the drive along which he had come. He had never been to the house before, but he felt that he

recognised it. It was just the kind of house he had
visualised during the day, while moving by furtive
stages towards it, and timing the stages to a nicety.
The Negro was not a master of psychology, though
he was a master of many other things, but he
judged this house to be just the right sort of setting
for what he had planned to take place in it ; and
the same applied to the fretful weather itself. He
saw himself in a picture, and his vanity enjoyed
the figure he cut in it. A dominant figure, quiet,
confident, unperturbed by the elements, both
human and meteorological. A figure of unexpected
power.

He moved into the protection of the porch.
Although he only moved forward a few inches, the
house seemed to come yards closer. He no longer felt
the drizzle on his face or heard its rustle on wet
leaves. All he heard was the silence on the other
side of the door. He took a key from his pocket.
At this hour on the previous night, it had been in
somebody else's pocket, but no objection had been
offered when he had exchanged it to his own. Nor
when he had similarly exchanged certain other
objects as well.

He inserted the key and turned it. He pushed the
door open. He peered into darkness. Suddenly a
streak of light pierced the darkness, revealing a
portion of unfurnished, decaying hall, and a strip of
yellowed wallpaper uncurling itself from a wall. The
light came from his electric torch.

He turned and closed the door. Afraid ? Sure,
he wasn't afraid ! But it was pleasant to know that
the door was closed, and that, until he chose, he had
the inside of the house to himself.   Or very nearly to

himself. Nothing was here that he could not deal with.

Still treading softly, he began a swift tour of the house. First, the ground floor. He had soon satisfied himself that no trouble lurked in any of the rooms here. They were full of musty emptiness. Stairs went up and down. He decided to go up before going down. The bedroom floor—there was none above it—proved as satisfactory as the ground floor. Only the bathroom gave him an unpleasant moment. The door stuck, and as he shoved it inwards, lost one of its hinges. He toppled forward after it, and nearly ended in a stained tub. He sat on the edge of the tub, and chuckled himself back to serenity.

Afraid ? Sure, he wasn't afraid !

Now he went down the stairs, guided by his torch, right to the bottom. The basement smelt damp and mouldy. He thought he heard rats. It was just the place for rats ! Then he heard another sound. Something pattering—not rats this time. He played his torch upon the spot. Silver threads slid downwards through the ray. Rain was coming through a half-open area window.

He moved to the window and quietly closed it.

All the doors in the basement were open but one. The closed door was at the back. He crept to it and stood before it, listening.

He groped in his pocket for another key. He brought it out, advanced it towards the lock—he knew that door would be locked without any telling, sure, he did !—then paused again. A sound came from the floor above.

Quickly he replaced the key in his pocket, and ran

up to the ground floor. He stood in the darkness of the decaying hall, his ear cocked. The sound was repeated. It was a rap on the door. Or, rather, six raps. One—a pause—two quick ones—a pause—two more quick ones—another pause—and then the sixth.

The Negro grinned. He switched on his torch, went to the door, and opened it. Four figures crowded in the little porch, and one gave an exclamation as the Negro's large figure loomed in the doorway.

" How the hell did *you* get in ? "

" Oh, I got in," answered the Negro.

" You said nine o'clock—no earlier ! "

" Sure I said nine o'clock."

" And that the Boss would let us in. Stole a march on us, eh ? Where's the Boss ? "

" I'm the Boss."

He twisted the torch and threw the beam on his own face. The visitors stared, then abruptly entered, as though blown in by a sudden wind. There were three men and one woman. One of the men had a boxer's nose, another was tall and grave, the third was small and mild. The woman possessed the beauty of the night-club. The Negro slipped behind them and closed the door.

" What's this mean ? " demanded the woman. " And where's Kurd ? Is this a double-cross ? "

The Negro twisted the torch again, now directing it towards the woman's face. She blinked angrily.

" Kurd was the double-cross," he said. " *Kurd was the Boss* ! Kurd was for gettin' us all heah and tellin' the police. Sure, I heard him. And sure, I stopped him. Now I'm the Boss ! "

Once more he played the torch on his large, coarse features with unpleasant relish, and then walked into one of the empty rooms. The others whispered for a few moments, then followed him.

" Now, then," said the tall man, advancing a little ahead of the others. It was he who had first addressed the Negro, and who appeared to have been chosen as the spokesman. " What's all this mean ? "

" I'm goin' to tell you," answered the Negro, and told them.

He switched off his torch, and his smooth, cynical voice came through the darkness. They listened so intently that only the woman heard the dripping of the rain outside, and the occasional low moan of the wind, and the footsteps of ghosts about the place. She shivered, and it was she who, standing in the rear of the party, put out her hand behind her and gave the unseen door a shove, almost closing it. She felt at that moment as the Negro had felt a little earlier when he had closed the front door to shut the garden out. Only the woman was trying to shut the house out. Those indoor ghosts worried her.

" What a crew ! " she thought. " Why did I ever join up with them ? I wish I'd kept on with that fat millionaire and got under his skin. We might have been in the South of France at this moment ! "

The little, mild-faced man, whose disappointed parents had once wanted him to become a real parson, was thinking, " I suppose there's really no way of getting out of this sort of thing, once you're in it ? "

The Negro's voice paused.

" Well ? And what did you do after—that ? " asked the tall man.

" What did I do after that ? " repeated the Negro. " I took out the knife—I got it heah—and put a bread-knife in its place."

" With your finger-prints on it ? "

" Sure, there wasn't my finger-prints on it, not when I left."

" You wiped them off ? "

" And put somebody else's on. That softy under the table. He was lyin' there handy, sure."

" Did you leave him lying there ? " asked the man with the boxer's nose.

" I left him there," answered the Negro. " *I* didn't hide him in no cupboard ! " He shot the beam of his electric torch in the other's face for a moment, to enjoy his expression. " And I didn't leave him against no milk-cans, neither, Mr. Rodent, I don't think," he went on. " I left him under the table, near Kurd, lookin' like they'd had a quarrel."

" But unless you finished him off, too," said the tall man, " he'd deny it when he recovered."

The Negro paused. He was coming now to an awkward corner. The one point he was not completely happy about.

" How do you know he recovered ? " inquired the Negro, temporising.

" Well, that's what I'm asking ? "

" Sure ! But wait a moment ! I ain't come to that yet. There was Kurd's pockets. That softy wasn't comin' to till I wanted, if he was ever comin' to ! I ain't no fool, like some. After what Kurd had told me, I was int'rested in his pockets."

" What did you find in his pockets ? " demanded the woman.

She felt she had been silent too long. She was

afraid she would never find her voice again if she didn't use it. But she hardly recognised it. None of her sofa-companions would have done so. Not the fat millionaire, for instance, who had once remarked, in one of his least successful moments, " You've got a voice like musical honey, Baby. . . ."

" I found some keys in his pockets," replied the Negro. " That's how I got in heah. And I found a letter in his pocket, and I've brought that along, too. Say, was the Boss some mad fool, what ? He let Massa Mildenhall pull the wool over his eyes like I told you, sure, didn't he ? "

" Yes, you've told us," answered the tall man.

" Well, what do you know, lettin' him do it the second time ? " exclaimed the Negro. " The letter I brought along, it's from some foreign agent, I guess, and it say that damn' stuff ain't no good, but jest ordin'y dope ! "

" And the recipe ? "

" Same damn' thing. Same damn' dope. I reckon our late Boss got the dope all right, all right ! "

" Then—what was Kurd going to do ? " exclaimed the tall man, after a pause. " He knew he'd been sold ! "

" Sure, and he was mad, and so was goin' to sell us, too ! He had to be smart on somebody ! "

" Yes, well, let's hear a little more about *your* smartness," came the suggestion, this time from the ex-boxer. " You ain't going to sell *us*, Nigger ! What did you do after going through Kurd's pockets ? What did you do to that other feller ? "

" Oh, don't worry about that other feller," replied the Negro. " He won't worry nobody ! " Then he reverted to the truth. " But the police came along

too quick, so I had to leave by a window. Sell you?
Don't make me laugh! Why, didn't I telephone to
you all, and fix this heah meetin'."

"Yes, you did," answered the tall man, "and
we're still waiting to hear just why?"

"O.K. I'm goin' to tell you," nodded the Negro.
"There's that girl, ain't there?"

"My God, yes! What's her condition?"

"We don't know yet. We're goin' to find out
right away. Maybe she's dead. But if it was jest
ordin'y dope, maybe she ain't. And if she ain't——"
He stopped for a moment, and with another burst
of his intoxicating conceit, he switched the torch
once more on his face. "If she ain't, maybe she
knows where the real recipe is, to save us the
trouble of lookin' for it! Say, is there any flies on
yo' new Boss?"

He grinned, and shoved past them towards the
door. They made way, and prepared to follow.
But as, by the beam of his light, he reached the door,
he fell back suddenly, and a bullet from the hall
shot the torch out of his hand. Instantaneously,
half a dozen other lights glowed into the room.

"Any one who moves is dead," came Inspector
Davis's voice. "Better take it easy. The house is
surrounded, the girl's away, and you haven't a dog's
chance. Show 'em the bracelets, boys, while we
keep 'em covered."

CHAPTER TWENTY-SIX

UNDER NEW MANAGEMENT

A WEEK later Margaret Mildenhall opened the front door of her late father's flat, and found that the caller was Inspector Davis. She was still pale from her ordeal, and her eyes were tired and heavy. The inspector looked at her sympathetically.

" Is it convenient ? " he asked.

" Yes, quite convenient," she answered. " I thought for a moment you were some other visitors I'm expecting."

" Oh, then, I'd better call again."

" No, come in. You know them."

She led him into the sitting-room. When they were seated, she inquired :

" Have you any news ? "

" Nothing much, I'm afraid. I was wondering whether you had any ? "

She shook her head.

" I can't think of anywhere else to search. You're quite sure, I suppose, that none of those horrible people have got it ? "

" Quite sure, Miss Mildenhall," he answered. " You can be certain we've cross-examined them very thoroughly, but I judge more by their attitudes than by their words. They're as ignorant of the whereabouts—and the contents—of the genuine formula as you and I are. But I've an idea that I know why we can't find it, and why we'll only be wasting our time to go on searching for it."

" What's your idea ? "

" Quite a simple one. It doesn't exist." He smiled at her incredulous expression. " Don't misunderstand me. It did exist. But after the first attempt to steal it, your father may have feared a second attempt, produced a fake substitute in case the second attempt were made, and destroyed the original after committing it to his memory."

" That sounds very possible ! " she exclaimed.

" To my mind, it's more than possible, it's probable," he replied. " In which case we must add another crime to the already overcrowded sheet, though not one we can make the subject of a charge—the crime of having deprived the world of something very valuable."

She considered for a few moments. Then asked :

" But, in that case, wouldn't my father have said so, when Kurd telephoned to him that night."

" After you'd been kidnapped ? "

" Yes."

" I'm not so sure. It seems to me that, in one mood, he might have told Kurd the truth, and in another he might have been afraid to. Look ! Kurd was in a pretty ugly humour when he phoned to your father, and your father must have felt both confused and desperate. Mightn't he have thought that, if he'd told Kurd just then that he'd duped him a second time, Kurd would have gone off the handle, and taken it out on you ? "

" Yes—I see."

" And afterwards, of course, it was too late, for he never got in touch with Kurd again. Maybe it was something about that that took him up to Brackham ? However, we'll never know that now, and

perhaps it doesn't matter. How are you feeling?
You look a little better than when I last saw you."

" I am better," she answered. " I've got to be."
She gave a sudden little shudder. " I—I wonder
what would have happened if you hadn't come
along when you did ? "

" And I wonder what would have happened," he
said, " if that most unpleasant Nigger's four working
partners hadn't come along just when they did ? He
was about to enter the cellar, you know—we heard
him moving up to the door—and he missed the
shock of discovering that we'd broken our way in
before him. He ought to have smelt a rat when he
found the area window open. But that's been the
weakness of that little bunch all along—most of
them thinking themselves cleverer than they
really were ! "

" I'm grateful for your own cleverness, Inspector."

" Mine ? I've done nothing to shout about ! The
ones you've really got to· be grateful to are that
queer little bloke who led us the deuce of a dance
before giving us the right direction, and his smart
companion——"

He was interrupted by the front-door bell.
Margaret smiled as she ran to open it. A few
seconds later the queer little bloke and his smart
companion entered the room. . . .

At least, Milly entered it, but Simon suddenly
stopped short in the doorway and put his hand up
to his forehead. This was the first time he had seen
the room since his original visit, and he found the
moment almost insupportable. The inspector seemed
to dissolve, and in his place stood an elderly, grey-
haired man, with an odd, nervous manner. . . .

" Is anything the matter ? " asked the inspector.

" Eh ? No," jerked Simon.

The inspector just saved himself from committing the *faux pas* of answering, " You looked as though you'd seen a ghost." Instead he exercised the tact of saying a few innocuous words, and taking his leave.

For a few moments after the inspector's departure all three were tongue-tied. It was Milly who broke a little silence which, although awkward, was also somehow pleasant.

" I suppose you're wondering how to thank us ? " she said, with the disarming frankness that had first drawn Simon to her. " Well, for God's sake, don't ! "

" But—I've got to," replied Margaret, the ice now broken.

" Well, if you've got to, be sure you thank the right person—him——"

" Eh ? No ! Not a bit ! " interrupted Simon, flushing. " I'd have been utterly lost without Miss Brown, and she knows it ! "

" Miss Brown ? Who's that ? " asked Milly innocently.

" Milly," murmured Simon obediently, flushing more than ever.

" If you want the real truth, and nothing but the truth," went on Milly, " we were a lot luckier than we deserved ! The best that can be said of us—and the worst—is that we meant well."

" Could it also be said, do you think," suggested Margaret, " that once you take on a job, you stick to it ? "

" Like Nugum, we do," smiled Milly. " Anyhow, we stuck to each other ! "

" Which was a fortunate thing for me." Margaret turned to Simon. " Are you feeling all right now, Mr. Smith ? "

" Me ? Oh, yes, thank you," he answered. " I only got a knock on the head or something. I—I hope you're feeling better, too ? "

" Yes. It's been a—a queer experience for us all, hasn't it ? "

The inadequate words produced another short silence. Milly broke it again.

" Miss Mildenhall," she exclaimed. " May I say something ? "

" Of course," replied Margaret. " Anything you like."

" I'm not going to sympathise. It seems to me we're beyond that sort of thing. But I hope you'll soon be able to look forward, and not backward, and—get something to do. There's nothing like a job for getting one's mind off. Am I being rude ? "

" No—sensible. And now may *I* say something ? "

" Well, of course, too."

" What are *you* going to do ? "

" Oh, *we're* going to get jobs ! "

" Have you got any yet ? "

Milly shook her head.

" There's always the advertisement columns," said Simon. " We'll find something."

His voice did not sound too confident.

" You bet we will," added Milly. " And—if we can, you know—we're going to go on sticking together."

" I say, are we ? " exclaimed Simon.

" Well, aren't we ? " retorted Milly, and then

turned to Margaret, as woman to woman. " Don't you think, sometimes, that men are terrible idiots ? "

Margaret smiled back. The room of haunting memories seemed a little brighter. Life was returning to it, to sit side by side with the ghosts.

" Why give up your present job ? " she asked.

" What do you mean ? " answered Milly.

" Nugum Limited," replied Margaret. " Under new management. You suggested yourself, Miss Brown, that I needed a job, too ? "

Milly's mouth opened wide. So did Simon's. Suddenly Milly's eyes filled with tears.

" Do you know, this is the first time I've broken down," she said hysterically. " Would you mind very much, Miss Mildenhall, if you see two very silly people give each other their first kiss ? "

THE END